DEATH BY DINOSAUR

J. D. Mallinson

Waxwing Books, New Hampshire.

Inspector Mason mysteries:

Danube Station

The File on John Ormond

The Italy Conspiracy

The Swiss Connection

Quote for a Killer

Chapter One

The sun was just breaking through the clouds after overnight rain on the morning in early May when Inspector George Mason and his young Scotland Yard colleague Detective Sergeant Alison Aubrey turned off the M4 motorway towards the market town of Newbury, deep in the county of Berkshire. They had made a later start than expected, on account of a lengthy briefing from Chief Inspector Bill Harrington. It was already approaching noon by the time they pulled into the parking lot of The Roe Deer, intent on snatching a quick lunch. The popular pub was already quite full with local farmers attending a cattle auction, but the two detectives were soon able to find a table in a quiet corner of the lounge bar.

"What's your fancy?" the senior detective enquired, as they scanned the menu.

The young sergeant took a little time making up her mind.

"Cock-a-leekie soup, I should think," she replied, "with a roll and butter. I just love leeks, especially if they are country-fresh."

"I think I shall try the game pie," Mason said, elbowing his way to the bar to place the order, while also requesting a pint of Flower's Bitter for himself and a tonic water for his colleague.

"The Chief Inspector seemed more than usually agitated at this morning's briefing," Alison remarked, the moment he regained his seat.

"Bill Harrington's under a deal of pressure," he replied. "The Home Office is leaning heavily on him over recent kidnappings at fee-paying schools. The Home Secretary needs to be able to reassure wealthy parents overseas, particularly in the Middle East and America, that England is a safe place to send their children to be educated."

"Which schools have been targeted?" Alison asked.

"Three, so far this year, including the case we are now looking into. All of them were attached to City of London guilds, which established them with generous endowments in the Middle Ages. The first incident took place at Silk Merchants Academy near Stoke Poges in January; the second, at the Cornmillers School in Camberwell, occurred in March."

"I read something about them at the time in the national press," Alison said, "while engaged on a burglary investigation in Pimlico. But I did not study them in detail."

"According to Ted Brearley, the lead investigator at the time, who has since retired, Scotland Yard were completely baffled. Ransoms of at least a million pounds were demanded and eventually paid by the parents to secure the release of the victims, neither of whom, fortunately, was harmed."

"So you have inherited Brearley's mantle, George?" she remarked. "The Chief Inspector could hardly have made a better choice."

George Mason returned a quick smile at her vote of confidence, while tackling his game pie with good appetite. Alison sampled her leek soup tentatively, allowing it time to cool a little.

"Time will tell," he modestly rejoined, "if Harrington's confidence is justified."

A half-hour later, they were on their way again, using a minor road that took them through the picturesque villages of Kintbury and Crockham Heath, before skirting the Hampshire Downs to reach Inkpen. Passing through the village, set amid arable land and pasture, they took a right turn and pulled up outside a substantial Tudor mansion set in spacious grounds. A painted sign at the gateway read FLETCHERS. The two detectives emerged from their vehicle and approached the main door. In response to the loud bell-ring, there soon emerged the tall, balding figure of Graham Thorpe, the headmaster. He had been expecting them.

"Scotland Yard?" he genially enquired, offering his hand in greeting.

George Mason nodded curtly.

"Would you mind very much if we strolled the grounds on such a fine day?" Thorpe asked. "This is such a delicate matter, and walls have ears."

George Mason, for one, welcomed the suggestion, as an opportunity to stretch his legs after the long drive from London.

"An unfortunate business," the headmaster then said, sadly shaking his head. "It can only reflect on the reputation of our academy."

"Is Fletchers another guild school," Alison Aubrey asked, "like those targeted earlier this year?"

Graham Thorpe drew himself up to his full height and said:

"We were founded in the fifteenth century, during the reign of Henry V11. Fletchers made the arrows for the longbow men who were so effective in wars against the French."

"Such as Agincourt and Crecy?" the knowledgeable George Mason put in.

"Precisely, Inspector. But archers became less important in the course of time. The last war they had a significant role in was the Battle of Flodden, against the Scottish king James 1V. That was in 1513."

"Yet the guild survived?" an intrigued Alison Aubrey asked.

"Indeed, it did," came the reply. "Until the late nineteenth century, mainly because archery remained a popular sport well into the Victorian era. It still has its devotees today, I am pleased to say. We teach it here to the senior boys."

Saying that, he led his visitors through the gardens to an arbor with a well-established hydrangea vine not yet in bloom. Alison chose to sit on the rustic wooden bench, while the two men remained standing. A cricket match was about to start on a nearby pitch.

"The local police have already combed the area thoroughly," Graham Thorpe then said. "They discovered very little."

"Describe the circumstances for us, headmaster," George Mason said, "as fully as you can."

"The missing boy is named Timothy Tuttle, aged fourteen. His father, William Tuttle, manages a hedge fund in New York; his mother Miriam is a dietician. Their son has been with us only since September, and now this."

"His parents will be devastated," a sympathetic Alison Aubrey remarked.

"Indeed, they are," Thorpe replied. "They are due to arrive here later this week, after taking time to redeem investments in order to pay the ransom. I have booked a room for them at The Fletchers Arms in Inkpen village."

"We understand, headmaster," George Mason said, "that the police need to keep a low profile in this case, as in previous kidnappings, to avoid physical harm to the victim."

"The monies involved have, I understand, already been wired to an account in the British Virgin Islands."

"Probably a shell company," Mason said, "whose beneficiaries will be very difficult to trace. Our main objective at Scotland Yard is to try to establish a pattern, on the assumption that it is the same perpetrator in each incident."

"From the fact that the incidents have all occurred at guild schools, Inspector?" Alison asked.

"It is an interesting coincidence, to say the least," her colleague replied. "Could you explain to me, headmaster, the manner of Timothy's abduction?"

Graham Thorpe with a broad sweep of his arm indicated a large copse on the far side of the cricket pitch, whence came the sound of bat striking ball and animated voices.

"Timothy's class were at the time studying plant ecology, a type of field-work related to their botany course."

"Plant ecology?" a puzzled George Mason queried.

"It is the study of the different plants that grow in close proximity on any given patch of ground," Thorpe explained. "The students study the characteristics of each plant, such as leaf-shape and the arrangement of the petals. They then try to identify them in the instructor's flora."

"A most interesting study," the detective remarked. "The instructor's name, headmaster?"

"Brother Linus. He comes over twice a week from the monastery of St. Caedmon, on the far side of Inkpen, especially to conduct the field-work, in which he is an acknowledged expert. We are very fortunate to have secured his services."

"St. Caedmon being an Anglo-Saxon monk?" the young detective sergeant enquired.

"Precisely, Sergeant," the other replied. "The monastery was founded in the twelfth century with a grant of land from a local worthy, with the approval of Pope Lucius."

"May we visit the site of the field-work?" Mason then asked.

"By all means," Thorpe replied, choosing a path skirting the cricket pitch which brought the trio within minutes to a minor road. Across it stood the large copse, mainly of oak and beech.

"Brother Linus allots a different plot to each student," he continued. "They are well spaced out, to cover as wide an area as possible. The results are collated over time to note any changes in the woodland flora. In these days of climate change, Linus felt this was particularly important."

"So the boys would not have much contact with each other in the course of their field-work?" Alison asked.

"They would be relatively isolated," Thorpe agreed, "making it easier to effect an abduction."

"With a speedy get-away by car?" George Mason suggested.

"That, unfortunately, seems to have been the case," the headmaster agreed.

An intrigued George Mason penetrated farther into the copse, noting the prevalence of ferns and bluebells among the different species of plants he would be hard put to identify, even with Brother Linus's flora. Something caught his eye. He reached down, picked it up and examined it.

"What have you got there, Inspector?" Alison Aubrey asked.

"A cigarette lighter," he replied, examining the brand. "It says DjEEP, Paris. Apparently of French make." He wrapped it loosely in tissue and placed it in his pocket.

"Could it belong to one of the boys, headmaster?" Alison asked.

For the first time in the present company, Graham Thorpe essayed a broad grin.

"Smoking is not permitted at Fletchers," he replied. "Brother Linus sometimes smokes a pipe, but never in the presence of the boys. I have never seen him with a lighter, to tell the truth. He prefers matches."

"Pipe smokers generally do," Mason observed.

"If you have now satisfied yourselves with the circumstances of the abduction," Thorpe then said, "we can offer you some light refreshment in the guest room. Tea with scones and homemade jam."

"That is most considerate of you, headmaster," the senior detective replied, a sentiment quickly seconded by his colleague.

Once comfortably seated indoors, Alison did the honors of pouring the tea, as her colleague buttered a scone and added strawberry jam. Graham Thorpe did likewise. They occupied themselves with the refreshments for a while, before George Mason said:

"Have you considered, headmaster, that this could be an inside job?"

Graham Thorpe shifted uneasily in his seat, sipped his tea and replied:

"What makes you ask that, Inspector?"

"Wouldn't it take an insider, someone with knowledge of the school routine, to know that Timothy's class would be out in the copse studying plant ecology on that particular afternoon?"

"You have a point there, Inspector," came the reply. "But I would be loath to consider the possibility. We are such a close-knit community here at Fletchers, which makes it very difficult to suspect any member of the teaching or ancillary staff."

"By ancillary staff, you mean catering, gardening, maintenance workers and the like?" Alison Aubrey asked.

The headmaster nodded, adding:

"All of them were hired with good references."

"Has any member of the teaching or ancillary staff left your employ recently?" Mason pointedly asked.

"One of the kitchen staff retired last month," Thorpe replied, "on attaining her sixty-fifth birthday."

"Our next step then, Mr. Thorpe," Mason continued, "will be to interview all members of staff. Detective Sergeant Aubrey and I shall review our other commitments at Scotland Yard before contacting you by telephone to make the necessary arrangements. You can expect to hear from us again within the next few days."

"We are in your good hands, Inspector," the other replied, as the two detectives finished their snack and rose to leave. "We are most grateful for your services."

*

Later that same day, the Hansa Lines ship *Bremerhaven* eased it way from the quay at Hamburg and slid slowly out to the North Sea on its way to the French port of Cherbourg, via Antwerp and Southhampton, before heading out across the Atlantic. On the foredeck stood a man in his early forties, gazing at the skyline of the historic city, which he had never before visited. He had arrived there earlier that day by train from Bad Harzheim, a spa town in central Germany situated at the northern foot of the Harz Mountains. Switching his gaze away from the city towards the docks, he noted a huge freighter on the opposite wharf, recognizing it as the Maersk Lines Triple-E, the largest container vessel in the world that had recently been featured in the German press. It was said to be longer than the Eiffel Tower was tall, with a capacity of 18,000 containers. It would be loading up, he surmised, with European exports destined for China, and would return with imports from that country. A marvel of marine engineering, he concluded, as he continued strolling the deck to sharpen his appetite for dinner.

One hour later, after freshening up in his cabin, Brendt Schulz located the dining-room at just turned six o'clock. Each table, decorated with a red carnation, was set for four persons designated by cabin number. His table companions were already seated. They included an American couple and, he was pleased to note, a fellow-national of approximately his own age. Conversation, slow at first while they weighed each other up, perked up after the soup course.

"Did you enjoy your visit to my country?" Brendt asked the Americans, correctly taking them to be tourists.

"We have had a wonderful trip," the American replied.

"And we should like to come back again, to visit places we could not fit in," his wife added.

"Which parts have you visited?" Otto, the other German, enquired.

"We flew into Munich," came the reply. "After spending two delightful days there, we visited the Black Forest, Rothenburg and Heidelberg, before taking a Rhine cruise north to Cologne, where we stayed overnight. We arrived from there this morning, in fact, to allow us time to see something of Hamburg."

"A most interesting itinerary," Otto concluded.

"So where are you from, may I ask?" the genial American enquired.

"Hildesberg," Otto replied. "A medium-sized city south of Hannover.

"And quite near my home town of Bad Harzheim," Brendt Schulz put in.

"What a coincidence!" Otto exclaimed, "That makes us practically neighbors."

"Worth a visit?" the American asked.

"Absolutely," Brendt told him. "We have the Harz Mountains and the Harz National Park, a heavily forested area where we are trying to reintroduce wildlife such as the lynx and the capercaillie."

"A most worthy objective," the American woman opined. "We are trying to do something similar back in the States, especially with wolves and bison."

"We also have the problem of invasive species," her husband added, as they tackled the newly-served entrée of pork cutlets. "They look set, in some areas, to wipe out large numbers of our native fauna."

"I have read something about that in our national press," Brendt said. "You have the Burmese python, Asian carp and insects like the long-horned beetle that damage your forests."

"We spend billions of dollars a year tackling such problems," the woman said, sipping a glass of pinot grigio. "But the problems only seem to grow worse."

"Global warming may have something to do with it," her husband said.

"Amen to that!" Otto declared.

The meal proceeded to a companionable conclusion with dessert, coffee and liqueurs. Now well out to sea, the ship began to roll quite noticeably, persuading the American woman that she would feel better resting in her cabin. The three men transferred to the aft bar, ordered steins of beer and chatted together for a while before the tourist decided to join his wife. The two German nationals re-charged their glasses and continued in conversation, as the sky darkened for a seemingly starless night.

"Bound for England, France or America?" Otto asked Brendt.

"London, as a matter of fact," the other replied.

"Vacation or business?"

Brendt Schulz cleared his throat and took a swig of pilsner.

"I am about to begin a six-month stint at Scotland Yard," he said, with more than a hint of self-satisfaction.

"Scotland Yard!" the other exclaimed. "How interesting is that! Please do tell me more about it."

"I am involved in an exchange program recently introduced by Europol, to increase their capability in fighting cross-border crime."

"Things like money laundering and people smuggling?"

The police kommissar nodded.

"And you could add international terrorism," he said. "Europol, from its headquarters at The Hague, provides information services and facilities for tackling cybercrime, for example, to member states of the European Union. Its agents may also form joint investigation teams with national police forces, but they have no power of arrest."

"So your program is designed to facilitate cooperation between European police forces, by giving you experience of each other's methods?"

"Something like that. A British detective-sergeant should now be on his way to Bad Harzheim, to study our methods; while I am to report to a certain Inspector George Mason, to assist him manage his current caseload. I was selected, from among the many applicants from the state of North Saxony, partly on account of my grasp of the English language."

"*Sie sprechen Englisch?*" his companion said, seemingly impressed.

"I speak English fluently," came the confident reply, "after several years' intensive study. How about you?"

"I, too, speak fair English, having visited the country several times. My acquaintance with it began years ago at high school, when we spent part of the long vacation attending language courses at Torquay, a resort on the Devon coast. Of course, we spent most of our time on the beach, with both English and German girls, plus a few other nationalities thrown in, often au pair girls from Scandinavia and East Europe. Something must have rubbed off in purely academic terms, since we got very good grades in our final exams."

"You are returning to England on this trip?" his companion asked.

"Just briefly," came the evasive retort. "But come, my good man, down your beer and let us take a stroll on deck. I need some fresh air before retiring and also an opportunity to smoke one of the Danish half-coronas I bought duty-free."

With that, the kommissar emptied his glass with one swig and rose nimbly to accompany his fellow-national to the upper deck, where smoking was permitted. The young couple romantically gazing over the ship's rail, buffeted by a stiff breeze, soon went below deck. A crew member made a quick tour of inspection, securing some deck furniture before leaving the two Germans to enjoy the night air. The sky was heavily overcast, threatening rain. The sea was a dark, gray mass, with a freighter's lights barely visible on the horizon, somewhere north of Holland.

Chapter Two

Around mid-morning of the day following his trip to Inkpen, George Mason was summoned into the office of Chief Inspector Bill Harrington.

"What developments from your visit to Fletchers?" Harrington testily enquired.

"The kidnapping seems to follow the previous pattern," Mason replied. "We aim to discover a link between them. All the incidents so far relate to guild-affiliated schools."

"A curious coincidence, to be sure," Harrington remarked. "Some person, or persons, with a grudge against private education?"

"More likely they were targeted because the parents tend to be wealthy," Mason considered. "Private schools reserve some funding for less well-off families, in the form of scholarships and bursaries, but they rely mainly on well-heeled patrons for the bulk of their income. Events such as this are bad for their image."

"You can say that again," Harrington agreed. "Anything tangible to go off, so far?"

"The only piece of evidence is a French cigarette lighter, recovered from the area where the students were studying plant ecology on the day Timothy Tuttle was abducted."

"Timothy's parents are due in England later this week, I believe," his superior said.

"Graham Thorpe, the headmaster, told me that the ransom had already been wired to an account in the British Virgin Islands. William and Edwina Tuttle will stay at a hotel in Inkpen village, in the expectation that their son will be returned to them unharmed within a matter of days."

"Let us hope then, Inspector, that everything goes according to plan and that there are no last-minute hitches. The chief constable of Berkshire has assured me that his agents will keep a low profile. If the parents had, for some reason, been unable or unwilling to pay the ransom, the police would have thrown all available resources at it."

"The assumption being," Mason suggested, "that Timothy is being held somewhere in this country, perhaps at a location not very far from the school."

"More than likely," Harrington agreed. "If similar incidents in the past are anything to go by, he could be at a farmhouse in a neighboring village."

George Mason essayed a smile at his senior's turn of phrase.

"Now there is one other matter, Inspector, requiring your immediate attention."

"The Europol program," Mason said, aware that a certain Kommissar Brendt Schulz was due to arrive any minute by train from Southampton, after his overnight crossing from Hamburg.

"Take time to show him the ropes, Inspector," Harrington said, "and help him settle in. It will all be rather strange and unfamiliar to him, coming to London from a town in central Germany."

"I shall do my best, Chief Inspector, to make him feel part of the team."

"Allow him some initiative, Inspector, rather than merely being a passive observer of our policing methods. Perhaps you should even let him take the lead in selected cases. Who knows? You might learn a few tricks."

George Mason returned an ironic smile.

"The Europol program is a good thing," he acknowledged. "I am all for it, the idea being that we learn from each other."

"Since it is comparatively new," Harrington then said, "many people will be interested to see how these prototype exchanges work out. I know I can rely on you, Inspector, to give it your best shot."

"Your confidence will not be misplaced, Chief Inspector," Mason assured him, rising to return to his own office to clear outstanding business ahead of the kommissar's arrival. He had just completed a report on a break-in at a Knightsbridge jeweler's and drained his mid-morning coffee when his new protégé appeared on the scene.

"Kommissar Schulz," Detective Sergeant Aubrey announced, ushering the German officer into Mason's presence.

George Mason rose from his chair and crossed the room to shake hands.

"Welcome to Scotland Yard, Kommissar," he said. "Had a good trip?"

"The crossing from Hamburg went smoothly enough, apart from a heavy squall off the coast of Holland. Most passengers retired early to their cabins."

"That does not surprise me," Mason said. "The North Sea can be very rough at times."

"Don't modern vessels have good stabilizers?" Alison asked.

"The *Bremerhaven* is the latest addition to Hansa Line's fleet," the newcomer said. "It is well-equipped for the trans-Atlantic route."

"Bound for New York?" the young sergeant asked.

"Boston, as a matter of fact," came the reply. "New York is already well-served by Cunard Lines."

"I expect you will want to freshen up after your journey," George Mason then said. "Your official duties here do not start until tomorrow, when you shall attend a briefing in this office promptly at nine o'clock. Lodging has been arranged for you for the duration of your stay at our hostel for police cadets at Maida Vale. The accommodation is fairly basic, but clean and comfortable, with a canteen for meals, unless you prefer to eat in local restaurants. They also have a gym and a swimming pool."

"Maida Vale has a variety of ethnic restaurants," Alison put in. "French, Italian, Chinese, Thai, you name it."

"It all sounds ideal," the newcomer said.

As the detective sergeant was summoned to the main office to answer a telephone call, George Mason grabbed one of the German officer's two valises and led the way out of the building. They crossed the busy thoroughfare and entered Westminster Underground station.

"Have you visited London before?" the detective asked.

"Several times during my student days," came the reply, "but not in recent years."

"Are you familiar with our Underground system?"

"Vaguely."

The detective drew his protégé's attention to a large route-map mounted on the wall facing the booking kiosk.

"Each service is denoted by color," he explained. "Red is for Central Line; blue is for Piccadilly Line; green is for District Line, and so on. All you need familiarize yourself with for the present is Bakerloo Line, which is the brown one. It gives you a direct connection to Westminster, without changing trains."

"Where the different lines intersect on this map means that you can change trains?" the other asked.

"Correct," Mason said. "You will soon get the hang of things, especially as we start moving round London in the course of our enquiries. I almost invariably use the tube, as we call it, on account of traffic snarl-ups."

"Many European cities are promoting bicycle travel for that very reason," the visiting German said, while thanking the English officer for his useful explanation.

"Including London," Mason said. "And, apparently, New York."

"Besides reducing congestion, it also reduces pollution."

"A good point, Kommissar," George Mason agreed. "And a very necessary one, too."

With that, he bought two tickets to Maida Vale and led the way by escalator to the northbound platform. Twenty minutes later, they reached the police hostel, where the visitor was shown his accommodation. It was a simple bed sitting-room, with toilet and shower, but no cooking facilities. Its windows overlooked a small park bordered by poplars.

"Take your time to settle in," Mason said. "The warden will explain things to you regarding house rules, meal times and so on. There is a nominal charge for meals taken in the canteen. And, by the way, in the Metropolitan Police we address each other by rank."

"As we do in Bad Harzheim, Inspector," the other said. "I am very grateful for your guidance and I feel sure this bed-sitter will suit me perfectly."

"You have the rest of the day to yourself," his mentor then said. "Lucky fellow!"

"I shall make good use of it," the kommissar replied, starting to unpack his things the moment he was left alone, before setting out to explore his new surroundings in one of London's more up-market areas.

*

Immediately on arrival at Scotland Yard on the following Monday morning, George Mason and his protégé were called into the office of the chief inspector. They had spent time the previous few days revisiting some unsolved cases in various parts of the capital, mainly so that the kommissar could familiarize himself with Metropolitan Police methods as well as learn to find his way around using the Underground. Mason had spent an enjoyable spring weekend with his wife Adele, visiting friends in the Cotswolds; while the German officer had spent the short break visiting some of the better-known tourist sights, including the Tower, Buckingham Palace and Westminster Abbey.

"How is our exchange candidate settling in?" Bill Harrington asked, directing his gaze at the kommissar.

"Quite well, so far, Chief Inspector," came the reply.

"He is quick on the up-take," Mason complimented, "and should adapt to our routines very readily."

"I am pleased to hear that, Inspector," Harrington said, "especially since you have a big new case just come through this morning."

George Mason glanced towards his protégé, whose eyes lit up at the prospect of a major investigation.

"Tell me more, Chief Inspector," he urged.

"First of all," Harrington said, "I need an update on the school kidnapping case."

"I have made arrangements with the headmaster, Graham Thorpe, for Detective Sergeant Aubrey to drive down to Inkpen today, to interview members of staff at Fletchers." He paused to glance at his watch. "She should be on her way by now, in fact. The assignment will take her a couple of days to complete. I pre-booked a room for her at Sparrowhawk Inn."

"Excellent," his superior said. "Now both of you, please have a seat."

The two officers drew up hardback chairs facing the cluttered desk.

"I am assigning you both to a murder case that has just come in. The curator of the Darwinian Institute at Kensington, a certain Leonard Kidd, discovered the victim lying on the floor of the institute museum. He had been stabbed through the heart with the rib of a sauropod."

George Mason gasped. "What on earth is that, Chief Inspector?" he asked.

"Sauropods, Inspector, were a species of dinosaur active around one hundred and fifty million years ago," Harrington explained.

"The diplodocus, for example, is a type of sauropod," the kommissar contributed.

"I am still not very much wiser," George Mason confessed.

"Then get over to Kensington as soon as you can. The curator sounded very agitated and will be expecting you. The forensics team is already in place."

"Has the victim been identified?" Mason asked.

Bill Harrington consulted his brief notes.

"Professor Rainer Weiss," he announced. "According to Leonard Kidd, he is a visiting professor of pre-history at Wessex University. Apparently, rather prominent in his field."

"German, too, by the sound of it," Mason remarked, with a glance towards his protégé.

"The name seems to ring a bell," the German said, on reflection. "I may have read about him in the

German press, as involved in some kind of controversy. Unless I am confusing him with someone else."

"Leonard Kidd told me he was a controversial figure," the chief inspector said, "in the, to my mind, rather arcane field of paleontology."

"Which is the study of early hominids," Mason asked, "such as homo erectus and homo habilis?"

"Something along those lines," his superior agreed, rising from his chair to signify the conclusion of the briefing.

George Mason and his protégé took a squad car, to save time. When they reached the Darwinian Institute, a large stone building set back from Kensington High Street, they found the entrance cordoned off and two uniformed officers of the Kensington sub-division on guard. An ambulance was partly pulled up onto the sidewalk. On entering, they were met by the nervous curator, who led them through to the museum at the rear of the building, where they found the forensics team busy sifting evidence.

"Good morning, George," the lead scientist, Walter Stopford, said. "Glad to see they have put someone with broad experience on the case."

Mason returned an ironic smile at that remark, while briefly introducing his new colleague.

"A fine kettle of fish we have here, by the look of things," he said.

"Blood everywhere," Stopford remarked.

"A rather unusual methodology, too," the detective said, peering at a large object the expert was holding in a zip-lock bag.

"You can say that again, George. Never in my time in forensics have I come across anything like this. The rib of a sauropod is a pretty lethal weapon, judging by the wound inflicted."

Mason's brow puckered as he examined the curious object more closely.

"Does it yield much in the way of evidence?" he asked.

Stopford judiciously nodded.

"We have retrieved some useful fingerprints and also what appear to be two different types of blood sample. The victim's is at the sharp end of the object, but there is in addition a small bloodstain higher up, together with what appears to be a fragment of human skin."

George Mason pondered the matter for a few moments.

"You are suggesting, Walt, that the assailant might have snagged his hand on a splinter of bone, while delivering a forceful blow?"

"That is a distinct possibility," the scientist allowed. "Lab analysis will decide the matter."

"The unfortunate victim being a certain Professor Weiss?"

Stopford nodded, while saying:

"The paramedics have just placed him in the ambulance, for transfer to Hammersmith General Hospital."

"Let me know the laboratory results at your earliest convenience," Mason then requested. "Especially if you obtain usable DNA."

"I shall let you know in due course," the expert assured him, as the detective and his protégé followed Leonard Kidd into his office fronting the high street. The trio sat round a polished mahogany table, in the center of which was a small wooden sculpture of an ibex.

"Such a dreadful event," the curator began. "It has certainly cast a shadow over the proceedings of the institute."

"Can you elaborate on that, Mr. Kidd?" Mason asked.

"Over the past weekend," the curator explained, "the Darwinian Institute has been conducting its annual conference, bringing together some thirty experts in pre-history."

"By which you mean," the kommissar put in, "paleontologists and anthropologists?"

"Assuredly," came the reply, "not forgetting the many other types of expertise in this broad field. We aim to be as inclusive as we can."

"For example?" a curious George Mason asked.

"Paleo-botanists, paleo-climatologists, paleo-geographers and so on. There are quite a number of different specialisms in our field."

"To which category did the unfortunate Professor Weiss belong?"

"He was an acknowledged authority on paleo-biology," came the reply.

"When was the body discovered," Mason then asked, "and by whom?"

The curator suppressed deep sigh before saying, in subdued tones:

"It was discovered first thing this morning by the janitor on his rounds. It gave him quite a shock. The poor professor must have lain there all night. Our annual conference, Inspector, was rounded off by a dinner last evening, at which most attendees were present. I personally spoke with Rainer Weiss afterwards, over cognac and cigars."

"Did he convey to you any fears or misgivings?"

"None whatsoever," came the swift reply. "He seemed hail and hearty and in an upbeat mood. He was also excited about the new exhibits in our small museum. We recently acquired the wing-span of a pterodactyl and the skull of a brontosaurus."

George Mason, not quite sure what those terms represented, looked suitably impressed.

"I have an impression that the professor was a rather controversial figure," the kommissar said.

"Are you implying that he may have made enemies?" Leonard Kidd asked, as skeptical as he was surprised by the remark. "Even so, it is difficult to imagine an academic bloodbath."

The kommissar looked peeved at the implied put-down and glanced away.

"Rainer Weiss was certainly very forthright in his views," the curator went on, noting the German's slight discomfort. "As a result, he took a deal of professional flack himself. More than that I cannot say, since my attention is fully occupied with the day-to-day running of the institute. I am an administrator rather than a research scientist."

"The kommissar may have a valid point," Mason said, in his protégé's defense. "It is one avenue that may be worth exploring."

"Then I suggest you look through back numbers of *Paleo Papers*, a journal to which Professor Weiss contributed several articles in recent months."

George Mason made a note of the name.

"The victim's next-of-kin?" he then asked.

The curator crossed to his desk and briefly consulted a file lying open for quick reference.

"His contact in case of emergency, Inspector, was his wife Ilsa."

"Do you have her telephone number?"

"Hildesberg 277. It does not mean a whole lot to me, I am afraid."

"It sounds like a German or Austrian number," the detective remarked, turning to his protégé for confirmation.

"Hildesberg is a town just south of Hannover," the German officer said. "I know it well."

"Isn't that your line of country, Kommissar?" Mason asked. "I have the impression, from our initial dealings with Europol, that Hildesberg is also not far from your home base of Bad Harzheim."

The kommissar smiled in acquiescence.

"Quite so, Inspector," he replied.

"But you are not familiar with Professor Weiss and his wife?"

"As I said a few moments ago, Inspector, I have an impression that Weiss was a controversial figure. It may have been something I read in the German press. Other than that, I have no comment."

"Yet they are a prominent family on your home turf," Mason countered.

"In academic circles, that may well be," came the rather diffident response. "In my police work, I have had little contact with the academic community."

"Until today," the detective quipped. "In fact, Kommissar, you can become directly involved by ringing this number and conveying the sad news to Ilsa Weiss of her husband's death."

The German officer returned a bleak smile.

"As a fellow-national of hers," he said, "I appreciate that this unpleasant task would naturally fall to me. Should I ring Frau Weiss straight away?"

"Better wait till we get back to the Yard," Mason replied. "It may take quite a long call, involving travel and funeral arrangements. Much better if a fluent German speaker handles it."

"Is there anything else you need from us, Inspector Mason?" Leonard Kidd solicitously enquired.

"Run the security camera footage for the period immediately following your annual dinner until the discovery of the body," the detective requested.

"That would be between the hours of 8 p.m. and 7.30 a.m.," the curator said, accessing the screen.

The trio watched the accelerated recording intently. When it was over, George Mason said:

"Since the recording shows no prowlers near the building, we must assume it was an inside job."

Leonard Kidd reacted in dismay.

"You are implying, Inspector," he said, "that the killer was present at the dinner?"

The detective gravely nodded.

"I shall need a complete list of everyone present at the institute yesterday evening. Include catering staff and other ancillary workers, as well as academic guests. You can fax it through to my office later today, using this number."

"I can certainly do that for you, Inspector," the curator promised, evidently disturbed at the notion of an inside job.

That said, the two policemen rose to take their leave, returning directly to Westminster. George Mason poured fresh coffee while they reviewed the morning's events.

"Chief Inspector Harrington," he began, "seems keen to allow you some initiative during the time you spend with us, and I am prepared to go along with that."

The kommissar sipped his coffee with a rather surprised expression on his shrewd features.

"That is very considerate of the chief inspector," he remarked.

"Not his most obvious quality," Mason quipped. "However that may be, I should be interested to know how would you approach the current investigation, based on what we have learned so far today?"

Saying that, he left his protégé to ponder the matter for a few moments, while he had a quick word with Alison Aubrey in the general office.

"We need to discover a motive," the German officer said, the moment his mentor reappeared. "I think a good place to look would be in the field of academic rivalries. Many experts have strong, entrenched opinions, which they will go to great lengths to defend."

"A good point, Kommissar," George Mason allowed, "based on the notion that Rainer Weiss was a controversial figure, as much in Germany as in England?"

The other nodded.

"So where do you propose we make a start?"

"The curator, Mr. Kidd, has given us a pointer in that direction."

"The *Paleo Papers*?" Mason said, nodding judiciously. "That may well prove a useful line of inquiry."

"Where would I turn up back numbers?" his protégé asked.

"Grab a bite of lunch in the staff canteen first," Mason replied, "then walk over to Westminster Public Library. They keep back issues of most publications in English. Enquire at the information desk and spend the next couple of days doing detailed research, after which I shall expect a written report. I shall be interested to see what you come up with."

Chapter Three

That same morning, Detective Sergeant Aubrey headed out early along the M4 motorway, exiting at Kintbury to follow the country road skirting the Hampshire Downs towards Inkpen. She reached Fletchers mid-morning, to be greeted by the headmaster, Graham Thorpe. He had arranged a series of interviews with the teaching staff to coincide with their free periods, allowing her use of the school library for the purpose. It was quite a tricky assignment for the young detective, aiming to establish precisely where each staff member was on the afternoon of the abduction, bearing in mind that the kidnapping was most likely an inside job. Most teachers claimed that they were in class, but several had been free of teaching duties at the time, citing a variety of explanations for their whereabouts. Some were engaged in lesson preparation; others in marking exercises. Two individuals were off the premises entirely, visiting the dentist and the local bank, respectively. Sergeant Aubrey spent a deal of time seeking corroboration of these accounts from third parties. By the end of the first day, she had satisfied herself that the teaching staff were above reproach, dedicated as they all seemingly were to the welfare of their students.

When school was over at four o'clock, she requested an interview with Timothy Tuttle, who had reappeared at Fletchers only the previous Saturday. He knocked timidly on the library door.

"Do please come in, Timothy," Alison said, indicating a seat by the window so that she could read his features clearly.

"I just have half an hour before my violin lesson," the boy said.

"That should be quite sufficient time," came the reply. "Have you been learning the instrument long?"

"Since my first year at Fletchers," he explained. "Next year, I shall be ready to join the school orchestra."

"Wonderful," Alison remarked. "Do you have a favorite composer?"

Timothy Tuttle seemed a bit stumped by the question.

"Not really," he replied, with a bemused smile. "I am currently practicing a sonata by Delius. I also quite like Mozart, when it is not too difficult."

"There's lots of great violin music you will discover in due course," the detective said, encouragingly. "Now tell me something about your recent adventure."

The boy shifted uncomfortably in his seat and gazed out of the window with a faraway look.

"Is the incident painful to recall?" she asked, with concern.

"*Rather,*" he replied. "It occurred while we were out studying plant ecology."

"In the local copse?"

The boy nodded.

"Two men wearing face-masks grabbed me and bundled me into their car, which then sped off away from Inkpen."

"About how far did they travel?" the young detective asked.

"Not more than an hour, perhaps."

"In which direction?"

"I cannot say, because I was blindfolded at the time."

"But you do recall much of the place where you were confined?"

"I think it was at a farmhouse," Timothy informed her. "A remote farm near a river. I could hear the sound of rushing water and there were odors of farm animals, but I did not see any."

"So you could not tell if it was a pig farm, say, or a poultry farm?"

"No, I could not."

"Is there anything about your abductors that you recall?" Alison then asked.

"Very little," came the reply. "Because I did not see them again until they brought me back to Inkpen."

"Who brought you your meals, Timothy?"

"They were left on a tray outside my door," the boy explained. "I think a woman brought them, because I sometimes caught a strong whiff of perfume."

"So you had virtually no human contact in several

days?" Alison said. "That must have been very distressing."

A pained expression crossed the boy's features.

"There was a television set and some adventure books," he explained. "I slept a good deal of the time."

"You survived, young man!" she then said. "That is the main thing. And you look none-the-worse for your ordeal."

"I was not mistreated in any way. Just very lonely and very anxious."

"And you recall nothing whatsoever about your captors?"

Something seemed to jog the boy's memory.

"One of the men spoke English with a foreign accent," he said. "I recall overhearing them speak in the car."

The detective sergeant noted that down, before checking her watch and saying:

"You have been most helpful, Timothy, and very brave. It is now time, I believe, for your music lesson, and I would not wish to delay you. Thank you for coming and good luck with your studies."

As the student quickly left the library, Alison Aubrey gathered her things and called at the school office to take leave of the headmaster, promising to return the next day to interview staff members employed in housekeeping and gardening. She then drove back down to the village, parking her car on the lot behind Sparrowhawk Inn, where George Mason had thoughtfully booked her a room for two nights. She was intrigued to discover that the building dated from the Tudor era, with the distinctive magpie architecture of alternating strips of black and white wood. On checking in, she found that she had been given a second-floor room with exposed ceiling beams and a four-poster bed. A sink with ornate hot and cold taps stood in one corner, but there was no bathroom en suite. She went back downstairs and mentioned the fact to the innkeeper, saying that she needed to take a shower.

"There are two bathrooms on each floor for the convenience of guests," he explained. "I thought of adding facilities to some of the bedrooms, but at an inn of this age the conversion costs would be prohibitive. We are a country inn, Sergeant, and most of our guests like it that way. We cannot compete with modern hotels in all respects, but our dining-room is rated one of the best in the county."

That at least was reassuring, Alison mused, as she made her way back upstairs and located the relevant bathroom, which she discovered had surprisingly modern fittings. After showering and relaxing for a while in an armchair by the window, from where she had a good view over the farmland behind the inn, she took a stroll to the outskirts of Inkpen to work up an appetite for dinner. The dining-room, she discovered on her return, was just an extension of the lounge bar, at which locals in farming gear stood drinking pints of ale or cider. She enjoyed overhearing their lively chatter, mainly about the weather and spring plantings. Occasional guffaws greeted the telling of a risqué joke, delivered sotto voce, out of earshot of the handful of dining couples. Following an ample meal of Wiltshire pork sausage, mashed potatoes and salad, she lingered at her table over coffee and a liqueur, while reading the London newspaper she had brought with her. As the evening wore on and the bar filled up with regulars, the louder volume of conversation led her to seek the tranquility of her bedroom.

Switching on the television to catch the late-evening news, her attention was immediately riveted on the report of a murder incident in London. She learned that a prominent professor of paleontology, named Rainer Weiss, had been found dead that morning in the museum of the Darwinian Institute, Kensington, following their annual conference and dinner. Scotland Yard had been called in to head the investigation. Inspector George Mason had revealed the unusual nature of the crime, of which there was no known parallel in the annals of criminology. The weapon used was apparently the rib of a sauropod taken from a museum specimen. Good old George, Alison thought. If anyone could solve such a novel crime it would be her redoubtable colleague, whose storied assignments had taken him the length and breadth of Europe. But what on earth was a sauropod, she wondered, as she switched channels to watch a movie before retiring?

On the following day, after a robust country breakfast, she returned to Fletchers to complete her round of interviews. She met some reluctance from the kitchen staff, who resented being interrupted during preparations for the school lunch. Feminine tact and persuasion eventually overcame their resistance, while eliciting little in the way of useful information. At the time Timothy's class were out studying plant ecology, the handful of kitchen workers were enjoying a late lunch together, as they customarily did after serving the students and clearing up after them. They vouched for each other's presence and were unaware of any events beyond their immediate ken. The young sergeant had more success with the gardener, Albert Cole. He claimed to have seen a black sedan accelerate rapidly down the road by the copse. The noise of the car's engine had distracted him from his work pruning fruit-trees in the school orchard.

"In which direction was the vehicle headed?" the detective asked him.

"Eastwards, towards Crockham Heath," he informed her, while unable to identify the make of car.

"But you say it was a regular sedan, not an SUV?"

"A large black sedan," he confirmed. "Could have been a Mercedes or an Audi."

"Thanks for that, Mr. Cole," Alison said, concluding that the farm where Timothy Tuttle was held could be somewhere near the Hampshire Downs, an isolated area consistent with the boy's account and the length of journey from Inkpen.

Graham Thorpe called her into his office just as she was about to leave.

"I do hope your visit has been productive, Sergeant Aubrey," he said, with evident concern.

"I believe so," she replied, "in that we can fairly safely rule out involvement in the kidnapping by any member of your school staff."

The headmaster was gratified to hear that.

"So my hunch that it was an inside job was off the mark," he said. "That at least is most reassuring."

"Assuredly, Headmaster. And Timothy Tuttle, whom I interviewed yesterday, seems none-the-worse for his ordeal."

"Remarkably resilient, Sergeant," Thorpe agreed, "as the young tend to be."

"We shall continue with our enquiries," Alison then said, "and let you know of any outcome. These investigations often take a deal of time."

"I can well appreciate that," the other said, accompanying his visitor to the main door. "Good luck with your efforts and many thanks for your valuable time."

On returning to Sparrowhawk Inn in a steady downpour, she skipped her planned stroll through the village and remained in her room watching television, hoping for an update on events at the Darwinian Institute. The main coverage, however, concerned a shooting incident at the Canadian Parliament. At just turned six o'clock, she went down to the lounge bar for a glass of cider before dinner. The poor weather had deterred regular patrons, leaving her practically alone with the barman, who seemed eager to talk.

"Hope the weather clears before weekend," he remarked.

"Taking a trip?" the young officer asked.

"Wish I was," came the reply. "No such luck. Saturday is the occasion of our annual spring fair, at which I generally man the drinks stall. If the village green gets a good soaking, it will create difficulties for the tractors and heavy farm equipment on display. They will just get quagmired, as happened two years ago."

"I see your point," his customer replied. "Best of luck for a fine weekend."

"The elements have generally been kind to us in recent years, thankfully."

"I expect the fair attracts a lot of outside visitors," Alison said.

"Several hundred, on a good day," the barman replied. "It helps swell the village coffers."

"Have you noticed any strangers hereabouts, in the last few weeks?"

The barman shook his head, pensively.

"Not that I noticed, ma'am, to be honest."

"Unusual visitors to the inn, perhaps?"

"There was one bloke," he said, on reflection, "that used to drop in for a pint after work. He had a foreign accent I could not quite place."

Alison Aubrey was all attention, recalling that Timothy Tuttle had also mentioned a foreign accent.

"Was he a regular at the bar here?" she asked.

"Most days, if it was fine weather."

"Can you describe him to me?"

"Aged around forty, with a swarthy complexion, hazel eyes and a shock of dark-blond hair. I believe he had some sort of job at the school."

"At Fletchers?" the detective immediately asked.

The barman nodded.

"Never said much, mind you. Just bought his tipple and went to watch television. Haven't seen him in several weeks now. I expect he's moved on."

As the man moved to the far end of the bar to serve a new customer, Alison Aubrey sipped her cider and pondered his remarks, aware that this could be a significant development. But why, she asked herself, had not Graham Thorpe mentioned this person as being in his recent employ? The headmaster had told the two detectives that the only person to leave Fletchers in the past few weeks was a member of what were usually termed the 'dinner ladies', on reaching retirement. How curious was that omission on Thorpe's part, she mused. What would George Mason make of it?

As the barman was hovering in her vicinity again, she asked him if he knew the stranger's name.

"Oleg," came the immediate reply. "I recall it because it struck me as such an odd name, matching his foreign accent."

"Did he tell you his name?" Alison asked, in some surprise.

"No, ma'am. But I heard him state it over the telephone at least a couple of times, when the bar was quiet. He used the house phone near the bar quite a lot."

"Many thanks for the information," the detective said, with feeling, as she drained her glass and crossed to the dining area. Perusing the menu, she ordered locally-caught rainbow trout with wild rice. As she was feeling pleased with herself, she also ordered a half-carafe of Muscadet and drank a silent toast to George Mason.

*

Around the same time that Alison Aubrey was heading down the M4 motorway, on her way to Inkpen, a smartly-dressed woman in her early fifties was driving her Audi from her home in the leafy suburb of Unterwalden to the center of Hildesberg. She found a parking spot on Mainzstrasse, locked her car and visited the nearby pharmacy before entering a medium-sized building opposite the local bank. It was the headquarters of the Freiheit Partei. On arrival, she was met by her campaign manager, Werner Hess.

"*Guten Tag, Ilsa,*" he breezily greeted.

"*Guten Morgen, Werner,*" she replied, crossing at once to the coffee dispenser. "What is the format today?"

"I thought we could make a start by doing some work on your forthcoming speech to the United Auto Workers," he said.

Ilsa Weiss added cream but no sugar to her coffee before joining the campaign manager at his desk by a window overlooking Mainzstrasse.

"Trade union speeches are very hard to make these days," she replied, "given the parlous state of the economy."

"The car industry has always been a key issue in the state of North Saxony," Hess replied. "Your speech could very well offer inducements to manufacturers to expand production here, rather than in, say, Bavaria or the Ruhr Valley."

"You are talking about tax incentives, Werner?"

"That much at least," came the reply. "Negotiated wage restraint would also be helpful."

"That will be a difficult sell to the trade unions," Ilsa remarked. "But they might just go for it in return for long-term job guarantees."

The campaign manager agreed.

"You could also make a plea for economic stimulus by the federal government."

"That will not go down very well with the finance ministry," she replied. "They seem resolutely against printing money."

"Probably, Ilsa, on account of our experience with inflation in the 1930s, when one needed a suitcase of banknotes to buy a loaf of bread."

Ilsa Weiss returned an ironic smile at that remark.

"Deflation, rather than inflation, appears to be the more immediate threat," she said. "If not here in Germany, certainly with the French and the Italians, who are pressing for more stimulus from the European Central Bank."

"I do consider, Ilsa, that you could afford to stick your neck out on this issue. It is one thing to promote employment in local industry, with an eye to the state elections in July. But you must also, while campaigning for President of North Saxony, have an eye to the elections next year for Federal Chancellor. The media will be covering in depth your upcoming speech to the United Auto Workers, which will help bolster your national profile."

The presidential candidate sipped her coffee thoughtfully. After a while, she said:

"What other issues, Werner, do you think are worth raising in forthcoming speeches, not just to the car industry, but also to the utilities and the service industries?"

The campaign manager leant back in his chair and considered the matter.

"The environment," he duly remarked, "is always a major concern with today's voters, especially the younger ones. We don't want the Green Party to steal a march on us in that respect."

"I can appreciate that," she said. "What about the euro?"

"There is nascent support for leaving the euro zone," Hess pointed out. "But that is a very thorny subject it may be wiser to steer clear of until we get a better sense of public opinion on the matter."

"You are probably right about that, Werner. I personally think the currency union was a big mistake. The British and the Swedes were smart enough to stay out of it."

"More pragmatic, the British," Hess agreed. "Less doctrinaire. However, we are stuck with it for the foreseeable future."

"That seems to cover the major points for now," Ilsa Weiss said. "Get the speech writer to do her initial draft by Friday, at the latest. Soon as I have checked my mail, I am driving over to Bad Harzheim to have lunch with a new backer."

"A word of caution, Ilsa," Hess then said. "Make sure your backers are all above board. This will be a very tight race, with a strong challenge from the Greens. Any hint of scandal could upset the applecart."

Ilsa returned a rather disdainful look at that remark, as if she didn't need reminding of the high stakes in play.

"I have taken all necessary steps to avoid any scandal emerging, whether of a financial or personal nature," she replied. "The presidency of North Saxony has long been in my sights, since I first entered state politics twenty years ago. Do you imagine I would let anything stand in the way of achieving my ambition?"

So saying, she repaired to a small private office at the rear of the building, where she spent an hour checking her snail mail and e-mail, several items of which required an immediate response. At just turned eleven o'clock, she retrieved her Audi and headed south along the autobahn, reaching Gruenes Glass restaurant just before midday. Following an extended lunch with a prominent businessman and a visit to his machine tools factory, she arrived back at her home in Unterwalden where, on picking up the phone, she accessed a voice-mail in German. She poured herself a stiff drink and sank into a nearby armchair to absorb the news. Fifteen minutes later, having recovered her sangfroid, she tried without success to return the call. She then rang her travel agent and booked a Wednesday morning flight from Hannover to Gatwick Airport.

*

A little before noon on Wednesday morning, Detective Sergeant Aubrey arrived back at Scotland Yard, to be greeted by George Mason.

"Had a useful trip?" he enquired, as she entered his office.

"*Very* useful," she replied.

"And the accommodation I booked for you was satisfactory?"

"Quite delightful," came the reply. "The Sparrowhawk is a Tudor-era inn, with lots of atmosphere and a good table. I saw you on television, by the way, on Monday evening."

"The Professor Weiss incident?" he said. "One of the most curious crimes I have ever come across."

"Murdered with the rib of a dinosaur?" Alison incredibly asked.

George Mason nodded.

"The kommissar is advancing the theory that it is a case of professional rivalry gone seriously wrong. Feelings can apparently run very high in academic circles, if reputations are at stake. Major controversies are endemic; egos are easily bruised. I am prepared to buy into that theory, since Bill Harrington wants me to allow the German considerable initiative."

"So he is now pursuing that line?" she asked.

"He is, or should be, currently at Westminster Library looking up back issues of pre-history journals."

"That shows a good deal of initiative," an impressed Alison remarked.

"Actually, it is a tip-off from the curator of the Darwinian Institute, Leonard Kidd," her colleague said. "We shall let the kommissar have his head on this one, pending useful leads. This afternoon, he will drive down to Gatwick Airport to meet Ilsa Weiss off the plane."

"On the grounds that he speaks German?"

"Not only that," Mason added. "Curiously enough, they both come from the same region in Germany, over by the Harz Mountains."

"A remarkable coincidence," Alison considered.

"So what do you have to report, Sergeant?" her senior then asked.

Alison Aubrey gave a broad smile.

"Something very interesting," she replied.

"I am all ears," Mason said.

"I interviewed the school staff, including the ancillary workers," she continued. "All of them appear to be in the clear. I also met Timothy Tuttle, who seemed none-the-worse for his ordeal."

"Was he of much help?"

Alison nodded.

"He told me that they drove for about an hour from Fletchers, and that one of his abductors spoke with a foreign accent. He said he was confined at a remote farmhouse, which suggested to my mind the Hampshire Downs."

George Mason carefully weighed her words.

"You could be right about that," he said. "We shall get the Berkshire Constabulary to comb the area, since it is their line of country. Anything else, Alison?"

Before she could reply to his question, the desk telephone rang. She watched her colleague pick up the receiver and listen intently for a few moments. A smile spread across his intelligent features, as he turned towards his young colleague.

"That was Walter Stopford, from Forensics," he informed her. "The two blood samples retrieved from the sauropod rib are from two different people."

"The victim and his assailant?"

"It would appear so. Walt has extracted usable DNA, which means we have concrete evidence. Now what was it you were going to tell me before the interruption?"

"I have the name of a possible suspect in the kidnapping," she confidently replied. "I got it from the barman at Inkpen that an individual named Oleg was a regular customer at Sparrowhawk Inn. The barman told me that he thought the man worked as a chef at Fletchers. He had also not seen him in several weeks."

"That is most interesting," her colleague remarked. "Are you thinking along the same lines as I am, Sergeant?"

"That it is very curious that Graham Thorpe did not mention him when asked if any member of staff had recently left Fletchers?"

"Precisely, Alison. That is a very curious omission."

"How would one explain it, George?" she asked.

George Mason considered the matter for a few moments, glancing out the window at the traffic building up along Whitehall. At length, he said:

"There are, to my mind, two possible explanations. One is that the headmaster is himself implicated in the kidnapping."

"Surely not!" Alison protested. "That would be unthinkable!"

As her senior colleague's face was breaking into a mischievous smile, she realized with relief that he was not being entirely serious.

"The other possibility," he continued, "is perhaps more realistic. This Oleg might well have been an illegal immigrant. Thorpe would not wish to alert the police to the fact."

"Because he was breaking the law in hiring him?"

"Exactly," Mason replied.

"Why would a school such as Fletchers hire someone like that, George?" she asked.

"Because illegals are under the radar," came the reply. "An employer can pay reduced wages since he needn't deduct income tax or pay social insurance costs. Many private schools these days are hard-pressed for cash and may look at unconventional ways to save money. Hiring illegal immigrants is not all that uncommon a practice. Why, even Members of Parliament have been known to do so, for gardening, domestic and chauffeuring duties, for example."

"I expect you are right, George," Alison promptly allowed.

"The question now, Alison, is how to trace the man."

"Do you have any thoughts on that?"

"There can't be all that many Olegs in the catering trade," Mason considered, "even given the large number of Russians now living in London."

"Mainly well-heeled Russians, I should imagine," Alison remarked. "Oligarchs and the like in their Mayfair mansions."

"It is how the other half live," Mason wryly replied. "Native Londoners can hardly afford to buy property any more, which is why so many of them are living on houseboats on the Thames. But to return to your original question, I think you could make a useful start visiting catering staff agencies, while the kommissar and I concentrate our efforts on the Weiss case."

Chapter Four

The funeral service for Rainer Weiss took place on Friday morning in the Lutheran church at the Haymarket. It was followed by a buffet reception at The Schooner Hotel, just off Trafalgar Square. George Mason represented Scotland Yard, partly to pay his respects and partly for the opportunity to have a few words with Ilsa Weiss. The latter objective proved more difficult than he had anticipated. Although the mourners were relatively few in number, the widow's attention was almost fully occupied by her late husband's colleagues from Wessex University, as well as by academics who had frequented the Darwinian Institute. The detective latched on to the curator, Leonard Kidd, as the only person he knew in that august academic gathering. Ilsa Weiss, prompted by the kommissar, paused on her way out to exchange a few words with him, explaining that she had a return flight to Hannover at 4.09 p.m., so that she could attend an evening fund-raiser in that city. Mason got the impression that she was relying on her fellow-national to keep her abreast of police enquiries. He also formed the impression, mainly from their body language at the reception, that the two of them had met before. That did not greatly surprise him, since they were both from the same region.

The reception slowly petered out after her early exit, with just a handful of academics lingering over drinks to make the most of one of those rare occasions when they could meet and talk informally, away from conferences, seminars, formal dinners and the like. Mason left soon after Frau Weiss, having reminded Leonard Kidd of the list of conference attendees he had promised to fax to Scotland Yard. He caught the tube to Westminster, reaching his office by mid-afternoon, with the intention of reading his protégé's report, which had been left on his desk earlier that day. Mason was glad that there had been someone on hand who spoke German, allowing the kommissar leave of absence for the past two evenings so that he could offer what support he could to the widow and invite her to dinner on departmental funds. His protégé had readily accepted the assignment.

On scanning the report, he dropped by the chief inspector's office.

"I am pleased to note, Inspector, that you acted on my suggestion to allow our exchange visitor some initiative," Bill Harrington said.

"The kommissar is advancing a theory of professional rivalry," Mason explained. "He has spent the last several days, when not occupied with Frau Weiss, doing research over at Westminster Library."

"How did the lady react at the funeral?" Harrington asked, with a rare show of human sympathy.

"Not much emotion in evidence," Mason replied. "In fact, she struck me as very self-contained, business-like and anxious to get back to Germany for a fund-raiser this evening."

"Not much in the way of mourning, then," the chief inspector observed, with a wry smile. "Is the fund-raiser for charity?"

George Mason shook his head.

"I got the impression from Leonard Kidd, the curator of the Darwinian Institute, that she may be engaged in local politics. But he was not sure in what capacity, whether she is a candidate, a party official or a financial backer."

"Perhaps they were not a very close couple," Harrington remarked, "if the professor spent his time teaching over here, while his wife pursued an independent career in Germany."

"I have no comment on that, Chief Inspector," his subordinate replied, "except to say that Rainer Weiss was a visiting professor in paleontology, presumably here on temporary assignment."

Bill Harrington sagely nodded and perused the document George Mason passed across his desk.

"So what is the gist of all this, Mason, assuming you have read it in some depth?" he asked.

"The late Professor Weiss was involved in a serious dispute with a certain Ian MacQuarrie, a professor at Lothian University. It was conducted over a period of months, mainly in two academic journals."

"Which are?"

"*Paleo Papers* and *Annals of Pre-History.* Professor MacQuarrie claimed last fall that he had discovered the remains of a hitherto unidentified species of hominid."

"By which you mean an early forerunner of our own species, *homo sapiens?*"

"I do, Chief Inspector. The remains were apparently discovered in a peat bog in the Cairngorms. The event was greeted with much excitement from the Scottish academic community."

"From the fact that a new species had been discovered on Scottish soil?"

"It was a first," Mason explained. "Nothing of the sort had ever been found in Scotland before. It eclipsed to some extent the discovery of Lindow Man, an early member of our own species found in a pool of sphagnum moss in the north of England."

"So many people were predisposed, you might say, to accept MacQuarrie's claim?" the senior man asked.

"Both sides of the dispute drew strong support from within the academic community," Mason explained. "Scottish experts largely agreed that it was a new species, which was named *homo caledoniensis;* while specialists farther south, led by Professor Weiss, vigorously contested the claim."

"On what grounds, Inspector?"

"Carbon dating found that the Cairngorms skeleton was about 35,000 years old, contemporary with our own species, which arrived in Europe about 40,000 years ago. It was of very short stature, with a comparatively large skull. Rainer Weiss claimed that the relatively few bones dug up were not sufficient to establish the existence of a new species."

"That seems a reasonable point of view," Harrington said. "So how did Professor Weiss evaluate the bones?"

"He wrote that they were probably from a stunted member of our own species. The short stature could have resulted from a genetic defect, dietary deficiency, disease or some other quite natural cause. He did concede, however, that they could be from a member of a pre-historic race of pigmies."

"In other words, not a new species at all, but a variant of early humans?"

"That is my understanding, Chief Inspector."

"These academic disputes are quite fascinating," Bill Harrington then said. "They spend most of their time in ivory towers and come up with the most fantastic ideas. A far cry from bread-and-butter police work, eh? But do you consider, Mason, that what we have here is sufficient grounds for murder?"

"The dispute certainly grew very acrimonious over the last few weeks," Mason said. "So much is evident from this report. I think it would be worth my while to go up to Scotland and interview Professor MacQuarrie, to get his side of the story. Leonard Kidd told me that he attended the annual conference at the Darwinian Institute, where he studiously avoided Rainer Weiss. He apparently left ahead of the after-dinner speech, which may in itself require some explanation."

"Very well, Inspector," his senior agreed. "It will have to be a solo trip on your part. Detective Sergeant Aubrey is, I understand, pursuing leads in the kidnapping case, and I am transferring the kommisar to a different case for a couple of days, to help broaden his experience of Metropolitan Police procedures."

*

Two days later, George Mason arrived at Kings Cross station to catch the morning train to Edinburgh. Some years ago, it would have been the storied Flying Scotsman, an express service inaugurated in the nineteenth century, to take him down the scenic east coast route, via York and Newcastle, to the Scottish capital. In its heyday, the train was hauled by famous locomotives such as *Mallard*, holder of the world record for steam. Such thoughts occupied his mind as the long train pulled slowly out of the London terminus, reminding him of his engrossing boyhood hobby of train-spotting. Ordering a coffee from the passing trolley, he opened *The Times* newspaper he had bought at the station kiosk to occupy him on the long journey.

On arrival at Edinburgh Waverley in the early afternoon, he took a taxi to Queensferry, a town situated on the southern shore of the Firth of Forth. Lothian University was on a promontory overlooking the water, with the impressive Forth Bridge on the one hand, the Lammermuir Hills on the other. Stepping out of the car, he took a few moments to absorb the wonderful scenery of southern Scotland and the bracing sea air, before entering the university main building, an elegant stone structure set in extensive grounds. Having made an appointment for three o'clock with Ian MacQuarrie by telephone the previous day, he approached the enquiry desk to announce his arrival. He was fifteen minutes early.

"Professor MacQuarrie is just concluding his afternoon lecture," the duty clerk informed him. "If you would care to take a seat, I shall notify him of your arrival."

"Would it be all the same if I listened in to the remainder of his lecture?" the detective tentatively asked.

The clerk reacted in some surprise at the unusual request.

"I do not see why not," she said, "since this is a public university. The main lecture theatre is along the main corridor to the right, but please enter quietly."

George Mason thanked her, followed directions and occupied a seat on the back row of the theater, hoping to pick up something of the arcane discipline of paleontology. The professor was explaining to what appeared to be first-year students features of the Bronze Age. The inquisitive detective, whose own schooling had largely skipped pre-history to concentrate on the British Empire, was interested to learn that bronze, an alloy of smelted tin and molten copper, was first discovered around 3000 BC in the Near East, ushering in more advanced tools and weapons, while also promoting international trade. If he had hoped that the academic would mention his controversial find in the Cairngorms, he was disappointed. Perhaps that was too advanced a topic, Mason surmised, for the first-year syllabus.

"Inspector Mason," MacQuarrie said in greeting, as the students filed out of the theater. "What can I do for you?"

"Just a few questions, at this stage," the detective replied. "Purely routine."

"Come along to my study," the other said, ascending a flight of stairs next to the theater as far as the second floor. Entering the small room with a desk piled high with books, he invited his visitor to sit and promptly ordered afternoon tea.

"You have had a long trip, Inspector," he said. "I think a little refreshment is in order."

"I did grab a bite to eat on the train," Mason said, pleased at the courtesy.

"You mentioned on the phone," MacQuarrie then said, "that you are investigating the death of Rainer Weiss. A most unfortunate incident, without a doubt."

"That is correct, Professor. I believe that Weiss and your good self were not on the best of terms, to put it mildly."

"We had our differences, I canna deny that," the other returned, in his Scottish brogue.

"One of my colleagues at the Yard did some research on recent articles in academic journals," George Mason said. "Rainer Weiss mounted a strong personal attack on you, calling your integrity into question."

"Aye, and that's a fact," MacQuarrie rather sadly replied. "He was not one for mincing his words. He even at one point called me a charlatan."

"Over a certain discovery you made in the Cairngorms?"

"Aye, Inspector. I have established, to my own satisfaction and to that of many experts in my field, that *homo caledoniensis* is an entirely new species, co-existent with *homo sapiens* and Neanderthal Man."

"That is a big claim to make," the detective said. "Professor Weiss seemed of the opinion that your main concern was seeking international recognition for your own expertise, in particular, and for the prestige of Scottish academia in general."

The Scotsman gravely shook his head.

"He overstepped a line, certainly, with remarks like that. Perhaps it was his German background, I do not know. A British academic would never come out with the like."

"He had his supporters, I understand," Mason pointed out. "Experts who thought the bones you unearthed belonged to a deformed, stunted or diseased member of our own species."

At that point, the tea arrived on a tray brought by one of the catering staff. Ian MacQuarrie did the honors, pouring milk first, then tea.

"Sugar, Inspector?" he enquired.

The detective shook his head, gratefully accepting the warm drink since it was a cool day.

"In academic life," the professor continued, "disputes are commonplace, especially in a field like ours, where we are very often relying on fragmentary evidence many thousands of years old."

"I can appreciate that," George Mason said, thoughtfully sipping his tea. "It quite resembles police work in some respects. Random bits of evidence that we try to piece together."

The Scotsman chuckled with amusement at that remark.

"Aye, Inspector," he said. "We have quite a lot in common, you and I. But you would be hard put to appreciate the technical problems we have with our material, so I won't burden you with the details. Suffice it to say that I believe further digs, either in Britain or Europe, will confirm my thesis that we have a new species of hominid who lived right here in Scotland 35,000 years ago."

George Mason glanced at a large color photograph on the wall behind the professor's desk.

"Would that be a view of the Cairngorms?" he asked.

Ian MacQuarrie turned his head to admire it.

"Actually, no, Inspector. It is a view of the Pentland Hills, south of Edinburgh. Wonderful walking country. I sometimes take my dog Caspar there for exercise at weekends."

"My wife Adele and I like to go hiking in the Lake District," his visitor said, "when the opportunity arises."

"England too has its areas of great natural beauty," the professor replied, "even if not on quite the same scale as Scotland."

At that point, the desk telephone rang, allowing Mason time to frame his next question. After listening for a few moments to the exchange in attractive Scottish brogue, he said:

"I believe, Professor, that you attended the recent annual conference of the Darwinian Institute, Kensington."

"That is correct, Inspector."

"Did you, by any chance, speak with Rainer Weiss on that occasion?"

MacQuarrie drained his tea and replaced the cup with a clatter.

"No, Inspector Mason, I did not. We were not on speaking terms."

"The curator, Leonard Kidd, told me that you did not stay for the after-dinner speech. Can you account for your movements following the conference?"

"I left Kensington and took the tube to King's Cross in order to catch the night train back to Edinburgh. I do not like to leave Caspar alone for long periods; otherwise I would have stayed longer."

"Can someone confirm your account, Professor?"

MacQuarrie shook his head.

"I live alone with my dog," he replied. "I have a house here in Queensferry, overlooking the firth. My wife and I separated two years ago. She now lives at Pitlochry, in the Highlands."

"Let me put it to you straight, sir," the detective then said. "You had a strong motive for eliminating Rainer Weiss, who set out to undermine your professional reputation. I have only your own unconfirmed account of your whereabouts immediately following the conference. You could have concealed yourself in the institute museum, removed the rib from the sauropod and waited for your opportunity to strike."

The academic returned a look of disbelief, mingled with dismay. He rose from his desk and crossed to the rear window, which overlooked a public park. After a few moments, he turned and confronted his visitor.

"To view me as a suspect in this dreadful crime, Inspector Mason, is quite preposterous," he protested. "What tangible evidence do you have?"

"I am looking for DNA," the detective replied. "Are you willing to provide a sample?"

MacQuarrie returned a look of incredulity.

"Are ye quite serious, Inspector?" he enquired.

"It would greatly assist my enquiries," came the reply.

The professor paced the room agitatedly for a few moments, before regaining his seat.

"What form would it take?" he asked, guardedly.

"Nothing so dramatic as a blood sample," George Mason explained, extracting a small vial from his briefcase. "A small amount of mouth fluid will be quite adequate."

The professor seemed on the point of obliging his visitor, but finally shook his head.

"That is not something I am prepared to do, Inspector. I consider your request a gross invasion of privacy. Rainer Weiss made many enemies. I suggest you conduct your enquiries elsewhere."

The detective quickly replaced the vial in his briefcase.

"Now, if ye will excuse me," MacQuarrie continued, in business-like tones, "I have a seminar with my post-graduate students to conduct in five minutes' time."

George Mason regretfully took his leave, called a cab from the Enquiry Desk and returned to Waverley Station with the feeling that his trip had not entirely been a waste of time. It had placed the professor on the defensive.

Chapter Five

Four days after the funeral, Ilsa Weiss paid a return visit to London. She explained to her campaign manager, Werner Hess, that she had private business to attend to and would be gone for a few days. Hess demurred at first, it being a critical stage in the run-up to the election, requiring a prominent public profile from the Freiheit Partei candidate for state president. Aware that she had recently lost her husband, he allowed that she needed some space to sort out her affairs. He would concentrate his energies on the media campaign during her absence, particularly on the North Saxony television network. There was also speech-writing to attend to with the specialist recruited for the purpose.

The presidential candidate had driven from her home in a suburb of Hildesberg as far as Brussels, where she parked her Audi and booked a return ticket on the Eurostar, an express service through the Channel Tunnel to Waterloo International. The advantage, to her mind, of this mode of travel was that she would arrive plumb in the center of London, avoiding the transfer from Gatwick Airport. Already somewhat familiar with the subway system Londoners called 'the tube', she took the Northern Line to Warren Street and covered the short distance on foot to the offices of Whittier & Co., her late husband's lawyers. Arthur Whittier himself received her in his spacious quarters on the ground floor.

"My sincere condolences, Frau Weiss, in your tragic loss," he began, offering her a seat. "Have the police made any progress in their enquiries?"

"None that I am aware of, Mr. Whittier," came the matter-of-fact reply. "But it is early days yet."

"I heard on the grapevine that Inspector George Mason is leading it. He has a formidable reputation at Scotland Yard."

"I believe I met him briefly at the funeral reception," she replied. "Now, about Rainer's financial affairs?"

"He has not made a will," the lawyer informed her. "In which case, by dying intestate, his assets go to you, as his next-of-kin."

"How long will the legal formalities take?"

"Since your late husband was employed by Wessex University, probate will go through Winchester Crown Court," Whittier explained. "It will take several weeks. Fortunately, his main assets are fairly liquid. He lodged a list of them with me only last month. They include bank deposits and various investment funds which can be easily realized."

"It is a stroke of luck Rainer did not own property here," Ilsa commented. "He rented an apartment at Winchester."

"Very true, Frau Weiss," the lawyer said. "It could take several months to find a buyer for residential property, especially with the credit restrictions currently in force."

"Young couples are hard put to come up with a deposit," Ilsa remarked. "In Germany, unlike in England or America, rented accommodation is often preferred to home ownership."

"In green and pleasant England," the other commented, "we cannot live without our gardens."

Ilsa Weiss essayed a brief smile at that remark.

"We Germans have to make do with window boxes," she remarked, "for closeness to nature."

"Very colorful they are, too, as I have had occasion to observe while traveling, especially in Austria."

"Switzerland also, Mr. Whittier, if to a lesser extent."

"Now there is one other matter you should be aware of, Frau Weiss," the lawyer said, rather hesitantly.

"And what is that?" she curtly enquired.

"Your late husband had a life insurance policy."

Ilsa's face lit up, but her smile soon faded.

"But you are not named as beneficiary," the lawyer continued.

"Who then?" she wondered.

Arthur Whittier shifted uneasily in his chair, avoiding her direct gaze while tending momentarily to a vase of spring flowers decorating his neatly-ordered desk.

"That is not something I am at liberty to divulge," he replied. "It is a substantial policy underwritten by

Winterthur Versicherung, a Swiss company. The provisions are strictly confidential."

Ilsa Weiss reflected on the matter for a few moments.

"That is very curious," she remarked, with a wry smile. "Perhaps Rainer had a mistress, which would not greatly surprise me, given the state of our marriage."

"I gather you lived independent lives," Whittier remarked.

"You can say that again, my dear sir. Our interests diverged some time ago. Rainer was bent on establishing an international reputation in his field, hence his move to this country. I chose to make my mark in state politics. The separation inevitably affected our relationship."

That observation explained to the lawyer the lack of emotion on display at her recent loss. She had seemed to him, observing her closely, to be very self-contained.

"I shall keep you informed about the probate, Frau Weiss," he said. "Is there any other matter I can assist you with, while you are in London?"

Ilsa Weiss emphatically shook her head.

"I think we have covered everything for the time being," she replied, rising to her feet and crossing to the office door. "I shall call you from Hildesberg if there are any further matters to discuss."

"Good day to you, Madam," Whittier said. "And best of luck in the forthcoming elections."

Ilsa Weiss warmly thanked him and quickly left the building, retracing her steps to Warren Street station, where she took the tube to Bond Street. She had it in mind to visit some of the leading stores in the West End, to buy a few items of clothing for the forthcoming elections. It was already late-afternoon, giving her just a couple of hours to browse the latest London fashions and choose an eye-catching new outfit.

Shortly after six o'clock, she walked through the entrance of La Pergola, an upscale restaurant in the theater district. A man seated at a table for two near the entrance rose to greet her.

"You made it!" he said, as she set down the fruits of her shopping expedition to occupy the chair facing him, noting with approval the small vase of fuchsia in the center of the table.

"Sorry I am a little late," she said. "I had not figured on the heavy traffic. My cab was stuck for ten minutes near Green Park."

"The rush-hour," the man remarked, "is notorious in London."

"I should have taken the tube," she said, "except that I did not know exactly where the restaurant was."

"The important thing is that you made it, Ilsa," her friend said. "We can spend an enjoyable evening together."

He then poured two measures from a half-carafe of Malbec, as they perused the menu.

"I think I shall start with the mushroom soup," Ilsa said, "followed by beef Wellington."

"A good choice," her companion remarked. "I prefer minestrone soup, with Dover sole to follow."

"Are you ordering white wine, too, to go with the fish?"

"I doubt it, Ilsa," came the reply. "I once read in the newspaper that Frederico Fellini, the famous film director, had cod with red wine on his seventieth birthday. I have had red wine with fish dishes ever since."

Ilsa Weiss smiled.

"Each to his own taste," she said.

"You are here in London on legal business?" he asked.

Ilsa nodded.

"I went to see Rainer's lawyer, Arthur Whittier, this afternoon," she told him. "Rainer died intestate. It will take time for his affairs to move through the courts."

"That is, unfortunately, often the case," her companion remarked, as he sampled the newly-served soup.

"Whittier also informed me," she said, allowing her starter to cool for a few moments, "that my late husband had a life insurance policy made out to someone else."

"But he did not tell you whom?"

Ilsa shook her head.

"I am suspecting he had a girlfriend," she said, with an ironic look. "Perhaps one of his post-graduate students."

"Not necessarily," her companion observed, quite amused at the revelation. "It could be for a favorite charity. Or for some academic purpose, like an endowment."

"You may be right," came the skeptical reply. "In any event, we are not likely to find out any time soon."

When the main course arrived, they concentrated on their food, helped down with liberal measures of the Argentinian wine. La Pergola began to fill up with diners ahead of the West End theater shows.

"How do you rate your prospects in North Saxony?" her companion asked, nudging his plate aside after a satisfying meal.

Ilsa thoughtfully chewed the last bite of the beef Wellington and took a quaff of wine.

"Werner Hess thinks our chances are good," she informed him. "He says that the Freiheit Partei has a slight edge in the polls, over the Greens and the New Democrats."

"Opinion polls are not always very accurate," her companion remarked. "Is there anything that could upset the applecart at the last minute?"

"Werner is afraid of some scandal coming to light," Ilsa said. "Financial or sexual shenanigans, of the sort that crimped our prospects in the last state election."

"Do you share Hess's misgivings?" he asked, with a look of concern.

"You are well aware, my friend, that I do not. Everything is under control."

The waitress hovered near their table.

"I think we shall skip dessert," Ilsa remarked, with a glance at her companion for confirmation. "Just coffee for two, please."

"The Apollo Theatre is just nearby," her companion said, consulting his watch. "We have about half an hour before the show starts at eight o'clock."

"What is on the bill?" Ilsa was eager to know.

"*Murder in Three Acts*, based on a novel by Agatha Christie."

"Sounds good. I am looking forward to my first visit to a London theater."

*

Earlier that same day, on arrival at Scotland Yard, Detective Sergeant Aubrey sought out George Mason. She had spent the previous two days visiting some of the various employment agencies in the capital, in an attempt to track down an individual called Oleg, whose name she had obtained from the barman of Sparrowhawk Inn, Inkpen.

"No luck?" Mason sympathetically enquired, noting the rather despondent look on her face.

"Not so far, Inspector," she replied. "There are any number of staff agencies in this city. It is taking far more time than I anticipated."

"Well, Alison," Mason then said. "You can put your mind at ease. This fax just came through from Leonard Kidd, the curator of Darwinian Institute. I scanned it closely just before you arrived and there appears to be an Oleg Volkov listed as sous chef for their annual dinner on May 7."

With a gleam of satisfaction in his eye, he passed the fax to his colleague. She grasped it eagerly and read the names of the catering hires aloud.

"By Jove, George, you're right!" she exclaimed. "If Kidd had got his act together sooner," Mason said, "and provided this list when I asked for it, you would have been saved a deal of legwork."

The thought did not much trouble the young sergeant, so excited was she to make a breakthrough.

"All you need do now, Alison," her senior said, "is ring Leonard Kidd and ask him which agency he contacted for catering services on May 7."

With that, he turned his attention to studying the names of the academics listed on the fax, while Alison Aubrey returned to the general office to place a phone-call. The curator quickly provided the required information, whereupon she left the building and strode purposefully to Westminster Underground, where she took the tube to Queensway. A short walk down Bayswater Road brought her to the premises of Alpha Staffing. A receptionist greeted her, showing her into the office of a youngish woman named Nancy Timmins, who handled catering staffs.

"What can I do for you?" Ms. Timmins politely enquired.

The detective produced I.D.

"Scotland Yard!" the woman exclaimed. "Are we on the wrong side of the law?"

Alison Aubrey smilingly shook her head, aware that the agent might have guilty feelings about hiring illegal immigrants, as many employment agencies did, often unwittingly. But such matters were not the detective's main concern at the moment.

"I understand," she said, "that you recently hired an individual named Oleg Volkov for the annual dinner of the Darwinian Institute, Kensington."

"What precise date would that be, Sergeant?" Nancy Timmins asked.

"May 7."

The agent consulted her computer records.

"That is correct," she said. "Mr. Volkov was taken on as a sous chef."

"Is Mr. Volkov still on your books?" Alison asked. "I need an address or telephone number where I can reach him."

The agent regretfully shook her head.

"He left no means of contact," she explained, "not even bank account details for wire transfers, the method we normally use for paying wages."

"So how did Mr. Volkov receive his pay?"

"He arrived here on the Monday morning immediately following the Institute event and insisted that we pay him in cash. We have had no contact with him since that day."

Alison Aubrey pondered the situation, reluctant to return to George Mason without results.

"Do you, Ms. Timmins, by any chance hire catering staff for private schools?"

The agent nodded.

"We do indeed, from time to time, for such establishments as Eton, Westminster, Harrow and Haberdasher's Aske."

"How about Fletchers, in the village of Inkpen, Berkshire?"

The young woman regretfully shook her head.

"We only service clients in the Metropolitan area," she pointed out. Seeing the look of disappointment on her visitor's face, she added: "You should try staffing agencies in Reading, the county seat of Berkshire. That would be your best chance."

"Do you happen to know the names of such agencies?" the detective asked.

Nancy Timmins rose from her desk and took down a large directory from the bookshelf. After consulting it for a few moments, she said:

"County Staffing, on Thames Street, is listed here as servicing the catering industry."

Alison thanked her, left the building and made her way back to Queensway station, thinking that Reading was no great distance. She could reach it in an hour, with light traffic. With that objective in mind, she returned to Westminster, retrieved her car from the parking lot and headed down the M4 motorway. Just before midday, she reached the center of Reading. She parked her car and asked directions to Thames Street, where she soon located the offices of County Staffing.

The agents were helpful, but had no record of an Oleg Volkov, suggesting that she contact an agency named Hello, Mrs. Chips at Newbury, a Berkshire town not very far from Inkpen, where she had stopped for lunch with Inspector Mason on their joint first visit to the school. The agency specialized, she was informed, in providing temporary and permanent staff for academic institutions, namely private schools, colleges and teacher training centers.

The young detective now felt more confident, as she accessed the M4 motorway once again and drove the short distance to Newbury, reflecting on the curious choice of name of her target agency. Hello, Mrs. Chips was evidently a play on the title of the famous novel about boarding-school life, *Goodbye, Mr. Chips*, using chips in its culinary connotation of French fries. She recalled her own school days, where the lunch-time kitchen staff were called 'dinner ladies'. It being after one o'clock, she paid a return visit to The Roe Deer, to grab a bite of lunch, elbowing her way to the bar to place her order in an establishment again full of local farmers noisily downing pints. She missed George Mason's company, but that could not be helped.

The staff at the employment agency were most helpful when she arrived there at two o'clock.

"We did indeed recommend a person named Oleg Volkov to Fletchers," the director said.

"Did you take up references beforehand?" the detective asked.

"Indeed, we did," came the reply. "But they were written in German."

"So you accepted them, just like that?" Alison asked, in surprise.

"They seemed legitimate enough," the director said. "But we are not linguists, I am afraid."

"Do you have them on file?"

The director, a woman in her early fifties with prematurely gray hair neatly permed, accessed a filing cabinet and drew out two documents, which she passed to her visitor. Alison Aubrey scanned them closely.

"These references," she said, "seem to originate from restaurant owners in the Rhineland. They could be legitimate, or they could be faked."

"We would have no reason to suspect anything irregular," the woman said, a bit taken aback. "We also must act promptly. Our clients expect early attention to their needs, especially since they often have quick turnovers of staff, for one reason or another."

"When was Oleg Volkov hired by Fletchers?" Alison then asked.

The director quickly consulted her records.

"It would be mid-February. They hired him as a sous chef."

"Are you aware that he left their employ in April?"

"I certainly was," the director replied, "since we were approached to find a replacement at very short notice."

"You mentioned quick turnover of school staffs. Volkov's job seems very short-term. Do you have any knowledge of his current whereabouts?"

"I am afraid not, Sergeant," came the reply. "Rates of pay are often the problem at private schools. Soon as they find something better, staff tend to move on. Restaurants in coastal resorts are a big draw in the summer months. Employees get fairly good pay, plus tips. I expect Mr. Volkov went to somewhere like Bournemouth, Torquay or Weymouth for the season."

Alison Aubrey thanked the woman for her assistance and returned to her car in buoyant mood for the drive back to London. Inspector Mason would be much intrigued to learn that Volkov was linked both to Fletchers and to the Darwinian Institute. It also seemed, curiously enough, that he had worked in Germany, although his name was evidently Russian.

Chapter Six

George Mason, on arrival at his office the next day, was agreeably surprised to receive a phone call from Germany.

"*Guten Tag, Inspektor*," came the upbeat voice of Hans Weidman, head of the Bad Harzheim police.

"*Guten Morgen, Herr Direktor*," Mason rejoined, in his best German. "What can I do for you?"

"I am enquiring about our exchange officer, Kommissar Schulz. How is he settling down to your Scotland Yard routine?"

"Admirably," came the reply. "He is staying at our hostel for police cadets at Maida Vale, where he seems quite comfortable. He is currently assisting me in the investigation of a murder which took place in London recently. Chief Inspector Harrington has encouraged him to use his initiative, so I have allowed him to take the lead in this case, at least temporarily, to see what he comes up with."

"That is most gratifying to hear, Inspector," Weidman said. "It will be valuable experience for him. Many thanks for your positive approach. Please give him my regards."

"By all means," George Mason replied. "And how is our British exchange candidate doing at Bad Harzheim?"

"Very well indeed," came the reply. "Detective Constable Higgins is settling into our operations quite nicely, helping experienced officers. I shall give some thought to allowing him more initiative, as I think that is a useful idea on your part. Aside from work, he spends much of his time hiking in the Harz Mountains. I personally took him sailing off Sylt at the weekend."

"The large island in the North Sea, off the coast of Friesland?" Mason asked.

"Correct," the other said.

Lucky devil, Mason thought, but he did not say as much.

"Give the constable our best wishes," he said, "and keep in touch."

"I shall certainly do that," Weidman said, ringing off.

No sooner had the detective replaced the receiver than Alison Aubrey breezed into his office with a broad smile on her face.

"You look pleased with yourself, Sergeant," he remarked, as she sat facing him.

"I surely am," she rejoined. "I had a useful day yesterday over in Berkshire, visiting Reading and Newbury."

"Turn up trumps?"

"I discovered something which may prove very significant, George. I was directed to a catering agency at Newbury called – would you believe it? – Hello, Mrs. Chips."

"You are kidding me," her amused colleague replied.

"I am deadly serious," Alison said. "The agency informed me that they arranged for Oleg Volkov to work as a sous chef at Fletchers in February."

"You don't say so, Alison!" George Mason exclaimed, rising to his feet. "This is a real breakthrough."

"If we can trace him," his colleague replied. "Neither the agency which hired him for the Darwinian Institute, nor the firm at Newbury, have any idea of his present whereabouts. Mrs. Chips thought he may have moved to the south coast for seasonal work."

George Mason slumped back into his chair, with a slight frown.

"So how do you propose to proceed now?" he asked.

"The agencies I visited over the last few days have all agreed to let me know if an Oleg Volkov contacts them in the near future. I am assuming that he will be looking for work at some point, unless he returns to Germany."

"What makes you say that?"

"His references were in German, from prior employment at restaurants in the Rhineland."

"I remember you saying he had a foreign accent. I shall alert the German police about the matter," Mason said, "as well as all police forces in the United Kingdom. Since we now have the man's full name, he is very traceable."

"Let us hope for quick results," Alison remarked.

"Amen to that, Sergeant. Grab yourself some coffee and write up your report. I shall catch up with you later, after my meeting with Bill Harrington."

As Alison crossed to the general office, Mason glanced at his watch. There was time, he reckoned, to make one phone call before his superior arrived at nine-thirty. He dialed the number for Fletchers, Inkpen. The school secretary answered, transferring the call to the headmaster's office.

"Good morning, Inspector Mason," Graham Thorpe said. "How are your enquiries proceeding?"

"Moderately," came the non-committal reply.

"Timothy Tuttle has settled back into the school routine, after his ordeal."

"I am pleased to hear that, Headmaster," the detective replied. "I am ringing you about a different matter, a rather delicate one."

"What would that be?" the other cagily asked.

"You failed to mention, on our recent visit, that an Oleg Volkov left your employ only last month. You mentioned only the kitchen aide, an elderly woman who was taking her retirement."

There was an awkward silence lasting several seconds.

"It must have been an oversight," came the slightly-flustered reply.

"Did you deliberately fail to mention Volkov because he was probably an illegal immigrant?"

"I did not enquire into his status," came the more assertive response. "I relied on the employment agency, Hello, Mrs. Chips, to vet his credentials."

"But you must have had your suspicions about him," Mason said.

"The truth is, Inspector, that we cannot afford to be choosy. Finances are tight. Some parents affected by the recession have withdrawn their children. We asked the agency to find somebody who would work for relatively modest wages. Volkov fit the bill."

"What did you know of his background?" the detective asked.

"Only that he came originally from Russia, but had also worked in Germany. He prepared some Russian dishes, such as borscht soup, which were popular with the boys."

"He would presumably have become familiar with the school routine," George Mason then said. "For example, would he have known that Timothy's class were out studying plant ecology at a given time on a given day?"

"Volkov may well have been aware of something like that, after a few weeks working here."

"He could have made it his business to find out."

"Is Oleg Volkov now a suspect in the kidnapping?" Thorpe asked.

"Decidedly, Headmaster. He may also connect, in some way, to the death of Professor Weiss."

"I saw that on television," Thorpe replied. "Most disturbing and regrettable. Professor Weiss was a valued member of our board of governors. I received a call from his lawyer, Arthur Whittier, only yesterday. He informed me that the professor had named Fletchers as beneficiary of his life insurance policy, which is a considerable stroke of good fortune for us, given the present state of our finances."

"Congratulations, Headmaster," George Mason said.

"There are strict conditions to the bequest, however," the other added. "The money is to be used to establish a fund for the education of German nationals. Rainer Weiss felt strongly that German youth would benefit from an English boarding-school education. We shall be advertising bursaries in the German press during the coming months."

"Cultural exchange is always a good idea," Mason agreed. "One other point, before I ring off."

"What might that be, Inspector?" Graham Thorpe uneasily enquired.

"How did Oleg Volkov receive his pay? By bank transfer or in cash?"

The headmaster breathed an audible sigh of relief at such a routine question.

"In cash," he replied.

"Thank you for your assistance, Headmaster," the detective then said. "It was a serious mistake on your part not to mention Volkov to us, when Sergeant Aubrey and I came down to Inkpen. But I accept your explanation that you relied on the agency to vet prospective employees."

"I am pleased to hear that, Inspector," a relieved Graham Thorpe replied.

"The Berkshire Constabulary may be paying a visit to Hello, Mrs. Chips, however, in regard to their hiring practices."

On ringing off, he caught up with his protégé, who was having coffee and chatting with Alison in the general office. Chief Inspector Harrington came bustling through the main entrance, curtly acknowledging all present before disappearing into his own quarters. Minutes later, George Mason and the kommissar joined him.

"What progress, if any, in the Weiss case?" Harrington testily put it to them.

"So far," Mason explained, "we have followed the kommissar's line that this is a matter of professional rivalries or jealousies, however you wish to describe it."

"I am pleased you allowed the kommissar some leeway on this," Harrington said, with an approving glance at the exchange officer.

"I went up Lothian University to interview Professor Ian MacQuarrie," Mason then said. "No witness can corroborate his story and he flatly refused to provide a sample for DNA purposes."

The chief inspector frowned deeply.

"In that case, Inspector," he said, "he remains a suspect. How do you propose to proceed?"

George Mason glanced towards the kommissar.

"I shall follow up Inspector Mason's work," the German said, "by interviewing the other attendees at the Darwinian Institute conference and dinner on May 7."

"The curator, Leonard Kidd, recently faxed me the relevant list," Mason informed him. "You can collect it from my office."

"I shall make good use of it, Inspector," the other said. "Thank you."

"Opportunely enough," George Mason then said, "Detective Sergeant Aubrey has come up with a new suspect."

"Who might that be?" Bill Harrington immediately asked.

"One of the catering staff hired for the dinner, by the name of Oleg Volkov. He is now a key suspect in the kidnapping incident at Fletchers. But it may be difficult to tie him to the Weiss incident. Could be just an interesting coincidence."

"Temporary catering personnel move around a lot," the chief inspector remarked. "As you say, Inspector, it may be just coincidence. Worth looking into, though."

"I am convinced this is a case of professional rivalry, Chief Inspector," the kommissar put in. "Professor Weiss's published articles regarding Ian MacQuarrie's discovery in the Cairngorms were very antagonistic, questioning the Scotsman's professional integrity."

"A very plausible motive for crime," Harrington agreed, seemingly satisfied with the kommissar's line of thought. "Get on with it and good luck to you both."

With that remark he concluded the brief meeting. George Mason returned to his own office to hand his protégé the curator's list, aware that it would occupy the visiting officer for several days. He then caught up with Alison Aubrey, who was putting the finishing touches to her report on staffing agencies.

"You can hand that in later," he told her. "You and I are going to pay a visit to Wessex University."

"At Winchester?" Alison asked, pleasantly surprised.

Mason nodded.

"We should be there in just over an hour," he said, "depending on traffic."

The young sergeant promptly shelved her report and accompanied her colleague outside. They were soon enough heading down the M3 motorway towards the county seat of Hampshire, one of the most historic cities in England. As they turned off the exit ramp and approached their destination, George Mason pointed out the ruins of Wolvesey Castle.

"That was the residence of the bishops of Winchester, dating back to Anglo-Saxon times," he remarked.

"Preserved by English Heritage?" Alison asked.

"I do believe so," Mason replied, "in common with other famous ruins, such as Fountains Abbey in Yorkshire. Soon we shall pass Winchester Castle, the site of King Arthur's Round Table. The names of his knights are said to be inscribed upon it. And some early English kings, including William Rufus, are buried there."

"You are a mine of information, George," his impressed colleague said.

"Just general knowledge," he said dismissively, concentrating on his driving.

At just turned 11 a.m., they parked their car in the university precinct and strode towards the main building, where they were directed up two flights of stairs to the late professor's study. It was cordoned off with yellow police tape. A uniformed constable stood guard by the open doorway. George Mason showed ID and entered the room with his colleague. It was remarkably tidy, compared with most offices Mason had visited in the course of his duties.

Bookshelves lined the walls and the femur of one of the smaller prehistoric creatures stood on the window sill. A large framed photograph of what the detectives took to be a scene from the Harz Mountains decorated the wall facing the metal desk, whose contents were stacked in neat piles.

George Mason opened a folder marked 'Correspondence', assigning the one marked 'Invoices' to Sergeant Aubrey. What he discovered there surprised him. It seemed that the late professor had been engaged in a substantial line of business buying and selling a variety of fossils. Aware that prehistoric remains were Weiss's expertise, it still struck the detective as an unusual occupation for an academic, apart from the more normal activities of lecturing and research. The pile of letters were mainly from his suppliers and various clients. Mason scanned them quickly, before lighting on something very significant. It was a letter from the legal firm Norcross & Richmond, to notify the professor that legal proceedings against him would be entered at Winchester Crown Court on June 2, barely two weeks from now! The litigation was being undertaken on behalf of William Wrigley, of Basingstoke, over the sale of fossils of dubious provenance. They were listed as:-

Item One - the vertebrae of a lizard (Jurassic Period).

Item Two – the jaw-bone of a sabre-tooth tiger (Miocene Period).

Item Tree - the complete skull of an iguana (Cretaceous Period).

Damages were claimed in the sum of 800,000 pounds, the detective read, to his considerable astonishment. Other letters were from apparently well-satisfied clients, complimenting the academic on his rare finds, leading George Mason to conclude that Rainer Weiss also dealt in genuine antiquities as a cover for less-legitimate activities. Since some of the letters were written in German and dated over the past several years, it seemed to the detective that the business had been in operation for some considerable time, long before its owner had taken up the post of visiting professor at Wessex University.

"Amazing," he remarked, half under his breath.

"You talking to me, Inspector?" his colleague asked.

"Just sounding off a bit," he replied. "This is really something quite remarkable."

Alison Aubrey rose from her chair, to peer over Mason's shoulder.

"A court summons," she gasped, in surprise.

"Evidently, Professor Weiss had some very lucrative sidelines."

"And disgruntled clients, by the look of it. Are you thinking what I am thinking, George?"

"What would that be, Sergeant?"

"That we have here a possible motive for Rainer Weiss's death."

George Mason rose from the desk and paced the narrow room, glancing out the window at the imposing lines of Winchester Cathedral.

"Did you know, Alison, that Jane Austen is buried over there?"

"In the cathedral?" she asked, in surprise.

"I do believe so," he replied. "I read something about it a few months ago, perhaps in a biography."

"You haven't answered my question, George."

"That we have a possible motive for the crime, Sergeant?"

He resumed his place at the desk and pondered the notion for a few moments.

"If that is the case, this William Wrigley is probably not the culprit. He is pursuing his grievances in a lawful manner, through the courts."

"But there could be others who felt similarly cheated," the young sergeant said, "who may not have the resources to pursue legal action."

"Very true," Mason allowed. "However, Bill Harrington wants me to follow the kommissar's lead on this and develop the theory of academic rivalries. But you have made a good point, Alison. I suggest you take this folder home with you tonight and see if you can come up with anything representing a threat to the late professor."

"I shall gladly do that," she replied.

"What else have you turned up?" he asked, glancing at the invoices.

"This file needs closer study, too," Alison remarked. "There are large amounts of money involved, and it should help identify persons who bought fossils from Rainer Weiss."

"When you have done with them, we shall pass both files to the Fraud Squad. Some at least of these suppliers bear looking into. It will be for the Fraud Squad to sort out the legitimate ones from the crooks."

"An interesting kettle of fish, altogether, Inspector," Alison Aubrey concluded.

"You can say that again, Sergeant," he replied. "And a very useful morning's work. I suggest now that, while we are in this fascinating city, we take a stroll in the cathedral precinct, grab a pub lunch and visit some of the sights."

"I am all for that," came the reply. "I should like to visit the tomb of Jane Austen, one of my favorite authors."

"We should be able to fit that in, too," he rejoined. "I remember you saying you studied literature at college."

*

That same morning, Ilsa Weiss slept late. Rousing herself with strong coffee, she showered and dressed for the office in a gray two-piece suit, allowing herself time for a light breakfast of croissants and home-made jam. As she was about to leave her home in the suburb of Unterwalden, the telephone rang. It was Arthur Whittier calling from London. She listened carefully to what he had to say, before setting off in her Audi to downtown Hildesberg. On arrival mid-morning, she parked her car and visited the nearby pharmacy for her migraine pills, before entering campaign headquarters. Werner Hess rose from his chair to greet her.

"*Guten Tag, Ilsa,*" he said. "*Haben Sie gut geschlaffen?*"

"I slept very well, thank you, Werner," she replied. "In fact, I overslept, uncharacteristically. Rainer's lawyer rang just as I was about to leave, hence the delay in getting here."

"News from London?" he solicitously enquired.

Ilsa nodded.

"Good news, too," she said.

The campaign manager crossed to the small catering area and poured fresh coffee for them both.

"Did Whittier mention the law suit?" he asked.

"He informed me," Ilsa replied, with a smile of satisfaction, "that the law suit against Rainer has been dropped. Lawyers for the plaintiff, Norcross & Richmond, contacted him late yesterday to say that, in addition to dropping the case, no claim would be made against my late husband's estate provided the genuine fossils are returned to Russia."

"How did Russia come to be involved?" Hess enquired.

"The Russian Embassy says that the fossils in question – Whittier told me what they were, but I cannot recall their precise names – were illegally poached from the Gobi Desert. The Russians wish to exhibit them at the Narodny Museum in Moscow."

"Interesting," Hess commented.

"If the trial had gone ahead," Ilsa wryly remarked, "it would have caused a major scandal, widely reported in the German media. That would have been very negative for our election prospects."

"I see what you mean, Ilsa. Was that all Arthur Whittier had to say?"

"By no means," she replied. "He also mentioned that he was initiating probate on Rainer's estate. My late husband died intestate, which means that his assets will eventually devolve to me, as next of kin."

"Probate through the courts can take several months," her manager remarked. "The outcome will be too late for election purposes."

The presidential candidate returned a rather petulant look.

"Private assets do not come into the picture, my dear friend," she said. "As you well know, Werner, our funding is more than adequate to meet campaign requirements. We have already outspent our main rivals. My contact in London, with whom I had dinner at La Pergola, Piccadilly, assured me that he had several key sources of revenue in the pipeline."

"That is good to hear," Hess rejoined. "We have spent considerable sums on television advertising alone. Far more than the Greens, for example."

"To what effect?"

"According to the latest opinion poll, conducted by Soundings A.G., you now have a lead of five per cent over your closest rival. Given a margin of error of around three per cent, you are well-placed to become the next president of North Saxony. Among women voters, your lead is six per cent."

Ilsa Weiss slowly nodded her approval.

"You have done an excellent job, Werner," she complimented. "When we finally achieve the desired result, there will be several key posts vacant at the Stadthaus. I shall be needing, for example, a new director of finance and a communications manager."

"I shall be more than happy to serve your administration in whatever capacity you see fit," he assured her.

"But let us not – as the English say – count our chickens before they are hatched."

The campaign manager drained his coffee and returned a wry smile.

"Your work on the Ordnungs Kommission has helped your profile with the general public," he remarked.

"The Law & Order Commission? It was time well spent, if generally rather tedious."

"The figures on crime in the state of North Saxony are due out later this week. Advance notice from the statistician's office indicates a significant drop in violent crimes, such as muggings, homicide and rape, over the past twelve months. Figures like that, on the eve of the election, can only enhance your prospects."

"Good to hear that, Werner," she remarked.

"While on the subject of law and order, how is our Europol exchange candidate doing over in London?" her manager then asked.

"Satisfactorily, as far as I am aware. But I am not in touch with routine police affairs. I leave that to the Polizei Direktor at Bad Harzheim, Herr Weidman. He has informed me that the Ordnungs Kommission will begin reviewing applicants for the next exchange program in the fall. I told him that, if elected president, I would have to resign my post on the commission, for lack of time."

"You did, as I recall, play a leading role in the selection of Kommissar Brendt Schulz, to inaugurate the new Europol program."

"That is now water under the bridge," she replied, with finality. "Now, to work. I have two major speeches to review before lunch."

Chapter Seven

One week later, the kommissar presented the results of his recent enquiries to Bill Harrington and George Mason in the chief inspector's office. He was in an upbeat frame of mind.

"The evidence so far points firmly to Professor Ian MacQuarrie," he began.

"On what grounds?" Mason asked.

"Prime motivation," came the reply.

"You seem very keen on this theory of yours, Kommissar," Harrington remarked. "Yet professional rivalries are commonplace, I imagine, in academic circles. Egos are easily bruised. Reputations and funding, especially for research, may be at stake."

The German officer returned a complacent smile.

"I have now interviewed a number of people who

attended the annual event at the Darwinian Institute on May 7. Practically all of them were well-aware of the deteriorating relationship between MacQuarrie and Weiss. It had been developing over a period of months and came to a head on publication of a series of articles by Professor Weiss in learned journals."

"With reference to - so Inspector Mason tells me - a newly-discovered hominid named *homo caledoniensis,*" the chief inspector said, with some skepticism. "Correct me if I am wrong, but isn't finding new members of our family tree quite a rare occurrence?"

"Paleontologists are continually making new discoveries," George Mason interposed. "Why, only last week the fossilized remains of an enormous dinosaur were discovered in Patagonia. It makes *Tyranosaurus Rex* seem a mere stripling."

"Amazing!" Bill Harrington remarked. "So finding new species is not all that uncommon?"

"By no means, Chief Inspector," the kommissar assured him. "China, for example, is a virtual goldmine of rare fossils, particularly of the first bird-like creatures."

Fresh coffee was brought in at that moment, creating a temporary lull in conversation. Bill Harrington's right hand reached down to the lower drawer of his desk, whence he withdrew a bottle of Glen Morangie, his current favorite in single-malt whiskies. He poured himself a generous tot, without offering it round. The German officer's face registered a degree of bemusement at the practice.

"What support, Kommissar, can you give for your theory?" the chief inspector wanted to know.

"Several of the academics overheard heated exchanges between MacQuarrie and Weiss," the other replied.

"Were any actual threats made?" Mason asked.

"Not in so many words," his protégé replied.

"Then your theory is mainly based on conjecture," Harrington commented.

The kommissar remonstrated.

"A Professor Lloyd, of Cambrian University, will testify that he observed Ian MacQuarrie enter the Institute museum shortly before the annual dinner ended. He also told me that only a handful of conference attendees visited the exhibits. Since the dinner ended quite late, most people were anxious to get on their way."

"Did this Professor Lloyd himself visit the museum?" his mentor asked.

The kommissar nodded.

"He told me that, as far as he knew, Rainer Weiss was the only person remaining in the museum when he himself left. He said that Professor Weiss seemed particularly interested in one of the new acquisitions, exhibited in a dimly-lit area of the museum."

"What conclusion do you draw from that, Kommissar?" Bill Harrington asked.

"That MacQuarrie could have concealed himself and lain in wait until all but Professor Weiss had left the premises. He would then have had the opportunity to deliver the fatal blow with the rib of a sauropod."

Harrington and Mason exchanged glances.

"An interesting development, certainly," the chief inspector allowed. "What is your opinion, Inspector Mason?"

The detective drained his coffee and replaced the cup on the tray.

"It carries the kommissar's theory a significant stage further," he replied. "But I am not wholly convinced by the idea of professional rivalry."

"So what would you advise as the next step in this investigation?"

"We need to approach Professor MacQuarrie again," Mason considered. "If he will agree to provide a sample for DNA purposes, it will resolve the issue one way or the other."

"Would that require a return trip to Edinburgh?" his senior enquired.

"Perhaps, perhaps not," Mason replied. "Academics of his stature tend to move around quite a bit, attending conferences, seminars and the like. I shall give him a ring. It may be possible to arrange a meeting at some intermediate point."

"Good thinking, Inspector," Bill Harrington said, draining his tot of whisky and chasing it with the coffee. "I suggest you do that without delay."

George Mason and his protégé thereupon left the chief inspector. The kommissar occupied himself in the general office, joining Sergeant Aubrey, while his mentor placed a call to Lothian University.

"Good day to ye, Inspector Mason," the Scotsman greeted, on picking up the phone. "What can I do for ye?"

"It is rather important, Professor, that we meet again in the near future. I am wondering if you are heading south any time soon in the near future?"

The professor quickly consulted his diary.

"I am due at Midlands University the day after tomorrow," he replied, "to give a guest lecture on *homo caledoniensis.* We could meet for lunch nearby, say, at The Shipman Inn."

"Around noon?"

"Twelve-thirty would suit me better."

"Twelve-thirty it is," his caller confirmed, ringing off with the satisfaction that Birmingham was only an hour away by train.

Detective Sergeant Aubrey entered his office at that point, leaving the kommissar to complete some paperwork.

"What developments from your recent enquiries, Alison?" George Mason asked, aware that she had been engaged over the last few days interviewing people whose correspondence had been on file at Rainer Weiss's study at Winchester.

"I sifted the letters from the professor's more disgruntled clients," she explained. "And I managed to make appointments with two academics who had purchased fossils from him for their own university collections."

"Academics who were also present at the Darwinian Institute on May 7?"

The young sergeant nodded.

"In accordance with your notion that the crime was an inside job," she replied.

"What was their reaction when you confronted them?"

"They claimed to be appalled at Professor Weiss's death," she said. "While they were angry at deception and unprofessional behavior, by selling them fossils of questionable provenance, they vigorously denied any involvement in his death. They were mainly concerned to get their money back."

"The kommissar is still pushing his theory of professional rivalry run amok. Personally, I am skeptical, but the chief inspector is inclined to support his approach. Aggrieved fossil clients is another avenue worth exploring, especially if they were present at the May 7 event."

"Would you wish to interview these individuals yourself, Inspector?" Alison asked.

"My priority at this point," he replied, "is to meet with Professor Ian MacQuarrie again. Depending on the outcome of that encounter, I may wish to pursue your leads. A very interesting situation, this. I think there may be a deal more to it than meets the eye."

*

Two days later, George Mason took a morning train from Euston Station to Birmingham New Street, arriving at 11.45 a.m. He hired a cab for the remainder of his journey to Midlands University on the northern reaches of the city. A short walk brought him to The Shipman Inn, popular with students and faculty as much for its typical pub fare suiting student budgets as for its lively atmosphere. Mason felt relieved that there was no piped or juke-box music, as he ordered a glass of Banks's bitter from the bar and found a table by a window overlooking a stretch of lawn, one of the few pieces of greenery in a largely built-up area. Professor MacQuarrie showed up at just turned twelve-thirty, acknowledging the detective as he entered, before moving to the bar to order a light ale. He then joined Mason at table.

"Pleased to meet ye again, Inspector," he cordially announced.

"My pleasure," the detective returned. "I trust your lecture went well?"

"Champion," came the reply. "The audience was very interested in my account of the discovery of the new hominid, it being a first for Scotland."

Saying that, he scanned the menu, opting for a bison burger and French fries.

"I think I shall try the plowman's lunch," Mason said, rising to his feet to place both orders at the service counter, in the absence of waiter service.

"What was it ye wished to see me about this time?" MacQuarrie asked. "Not, I hope, this ridiculous business about DNA."

"I urge you to comply with my request, Professor," the detective urged, "in your own interest."

The Scotsman's face darkened a few shades. He poured his bottled beer into a tumbler and regarded his visitor quizzically, before taking a quaff.

"And why would that be?" he queried.

"We have a reliable witness who saw you enter the Institute museum immediately after the annual dinner," Mason explained. "Our view is that you concealed yourself there until the guest speaker had finished his delivery, lying in wait for the opportunity to attack Professor Weiss."

"Preposterous, Inspector!" came the response.

"What explanation do you have for your early exit from the dinner?" Mason challenged.

At that point, the service counter called out their table number. The detective rose to his feet and went to collect the order. The arrival of food eased the tension, as the academic tackled his burger with good appetite and George Mason embarked on his plowman's lunch of wholemeal bread, Cheddar cheese and mixed pickles.

Half-way through his meal, the Scot said:

"I did indeed leave the dinner before the speech," he admitted. "For one thing, I canna abide after-dinner speeches. They drag on so. As to why I visited the museum, the explanation is quite simple."

"What would that be?" the detective enquired.

"I told you before, Inspector, at our last meeting, that I needed to catch the night train to Edinburgh. Since my visits to London are generally few and far between, I took the opportunity to inspect one of the Institute's more recent acquisitions."

"Which was?" Mason prompted.

"An ichthyosaur fossil retrieved from southern China only last year. It was a very significant find."

"How so?"

"Because it fills a gap in the evolutionary record."

"How long ago would that be?" Mason asked, much intrigued by this unfamiliar branch of science, what with new hominids and giant dinosaurs coming to light in quick succession. He also aimed to establish a rapport with the canny Scot by showing interest in his line of work.

"About 300 million years ago," came the reply. "The ichthyosaur was an amphibious creature distantly related to reptiles. Its large flippers may have helped it walk on land, as well as swim in water."

"A sort of intermediate creature?" Mason asked, nudging his finished plate aside.

Ian MacQuarrie, appreciative of the detective's interest, warmed to his subject.

"In appearance it resembled a small dolphin," he explained. "And from living on land, it eventually returned to the ocean."

"I always thought evolution moved in the opposite direction," Mason said, "with creatures moving from the sea to the land."

"That was generally the case," the Scot confirmed. "But there are exceptions, which make my field of research all the more unpredictable."

"Most interesting, Professor," the detective commented. "So you studied the fossil closely and then left the museum?"

"I did, sir, in order to catch the train back to Edinburgh."

"Did you leave before the after-dinner speech ended?"

"I was there long enough to hear the guest speaker's concluding remarks, but I left before the other attendees rose from table. I assume that some of them then decided to visit the museum, for much the same reason as I myself did. Professor Weiss may have been one of them."

"He surely was," Mason asserted, "if he was later found stabbed through the heart with the rib of a sauropod."

The Scot returned a deep frown.

"A most unfortunate occurrence," he said. "I had no great regard for the man, personally or professionally, but I would not wish such a fate on my worst enemy."

With that, he nudged his plate aside and sipped his beer.

"You need to establish your innocence," George Mason then said. "Your account sounds plausible enough to me, but you have no witness to back it up. You also have a motive for harming Weiss, in view of the attacks he made on your professional integrity."

The professor sadly shook his head.

"*Somebody* obviously had a strong-enough motive to do him in," he remarked.

"The fact is, Professor," Mason then said, carefully weighing his words, "that Chief Inspector Harrington may, on the basis of the evidence we have, issue a warrant for your arrest. It would be very much in your interest, if you are truly innocent of this crime, to provide me with a sample of body fluid for DNA purposes. Our forensic department will then analyze it, to settle the matter one way or the other."

The academic considered the matter for a few moments, glancing out of the widow to admire a chaffinch perched on the bough of a silver birch. Eventually, he said:

"Ye seem to have me over a barrel, my good fellow. What precisely do ye mean by body fluid?"

George Mason withdrew a small plastic vial from his briefcase and passed it to him.

"Just go to the bathroom and deposit a small amount of saliva in this vial," he instructed. "That will be quite adequate for our purposes."

The Scot took the vial and rose from table to comply with the request. By the time he returned, Mason had fetched another round of beers from the bar, with the aim of extending the lunch-hour meeting to find out more about the professor's fascinating line of work. The professor was only too happy to oblige, describing in detail how he had come across hominid remains in the Cairngorms, before taking his leave at two o'clock for a meeting with the university provost. George Mason took the opportunity of calling on an old friend of his, Cedric Haynes, a former colleague who had transferred from London to the Birmingham Constabulary three years ago.

Chapter Eight

On arrival at Scotland Yard the next day, George Mason went straight to the forensics department and handed to Walter Stopford, the lead scientist, the sample he had finally persuaded Ian MacQuarrie to provide. Stopford explained that the laboratory was undergoing refurbishment, and that results would not be available until the following week. The desk telephone rang the moment Mason reached his office. He sat down and picked up the receiver, surprised to get another call so soon from Hans Weidman, the Polizei Direktor at Bad Harzheim. What he heard stunned him, making him wish that, in common with Bill Harrington, he had a cache of malt whisky in his bottom drawer. He felt sorely in need of a stiff drink.

"The body of Kommissar Brendt Schulz washed up on the island of Sylt, in the North Sea," the German officer informed him, in the gravest tones.

George Mason was speechless for several moments.

"Did you hear me, Inspector?" the director asked.

"Only too clearly," Mason said. "And I truly wish I had not heard what you said."

"I am so sorry to have to relay such terrible news," the German said.

"The question, Herr Direktor, is who on earth is this person masquerading as a Europol exchange officer?"

"That remains to be seen," came the rather shaky reply.

"If you are thinking along the same lines as I am," Mason said, "we have been harboring here at Scotland Yard an impostor, who is also presumably a murderer."

"Assuming that this person arrived in London at the scheduled time and place, he must have been aware of Schulz's plans. He eliminated our officer, took his place and you were none the wiser, Inspector Mason."

"Kommissar Schulz went overboard from the Hamburg liner?"

"That would seem an inescapable conclusion," Hans Weidman remarked. "I shall contact Hansa Lines and ask them to fax me without delay the manifest of the *Bremerhaven* for that particular voyage. I shall check all single, male passengers listed on it."

"This puts me in a very ticklish position, Herr Direktor," Mason said. "I shall have to go along with this deception for the time being. The impostor will not suspect that he is under suspicion, provided news of the discovery of Schulz's body is kept from the public."

"I can certainly put a moratorium on media coverage," Weidman assured him. "At least as a temporary measure."

On replacing the receiver, George Mason gasped and sat back in his chair to take stock of this very disturbing new development. In lieu of a stiff whisky, he poured black coffee and pondered the situation, aware that the self-styled kommissar was next door in the general office chatting with Alison Aubrey. He checked his mail until the chief inspector arrived, went directly to see him and relayed what Hans Weidman had told him. Bill Harrington's face turned livid.

"Arrest him at once," he urged.

"I am not sure that would be the best plan, Chief Inspector," Mason replied. "For one thing, we do not know exactly who he is. For another, I should like time to ascertain his motives for insinuating himself into our organization."

"What line do you propose to take?" Harrington asked him.

"I suggest that we put a tail on him, follow all his movements outside of Scotland Yard, find out whom he meets and why."

Bill Harrington pondered the situation.

"We could not track him from this office," he said. "He would recognize any officer from our department."

"We could bring somebody in from another force," Mason suggested. "I was in touch only yesterday with an old friend of mine, Cedric Haynes, who in fact worked here three years ago, before moving to Birmingham. You may remember him. A tall man, with wiry ginger hair."

"Vaguely," came the reply. "Very keen on golf, as I recall."

"He could recommend one of his staff to assist us. I shall contact him straight away."

"And what will you be doing while this shadowing process is taking place, Inspector? Business as usual?"

"Hardly that, Chief Inspector. In fact, I think you should transfer our German friend to a different officer, with the ostensible aim of broadening his experience of our methods. He will go for that and probably welcome the change."

Bill Harrington considered the proposal.

"I could assign him to Inspector Roy Greenhalgh," he said, "who specializes in fraud."

"Very appropriate, in the circumstances," Mason agreed. "Meanwhile, I shall take a trip to Bad Harzheim and find out what Direktor Weidman has to report. This must be very hush-hush, however. My colleagues must not suspect anything. Let it be known that I am taking leave of absence for family matters. I shall be back within days."

For the first time that morning, the chief inspector's face registered a glimmer of satisfaction.

"Good thinking, Inspector," he said. "I am counting on you to get to the bottom of this incredible business. Send the kommissar to my office and I shall act quite naturally, as if I know nothing, while re-assigning him."

"Oddly enough, he seems quite at home in a police department," George Mason remarked, "and knowledgeable about police methods in Germany, about which I have frequently asked him questions."

"Very odd, indeed," Harrington agreed. "The plot only thickens."

With that, George Mason returned to his own office, shut the door firmly and placed a call to Birmingham. Without going into detail about the reasons for his request, he persuaded Cedric Haynes to second one of his most able officers, Detective Sergeant Janet Midler, to Scotland Yard for as long as Mason saw fit. She would come down to London first thing tomorrow morning.

*

The next day, George Mason went to Euston Station to meet Detective Sergeant Midler off an early train from the Midlands. He found an attractive, petite woman with chin-length dark hair, casually dressed for the warm spring weather. Over coffee in the station cafeteria, he gave her the address of the police hostel at Maida Vale and a briefing to shadow the German wherever he went on his off-duty hours, evenings and weekend. Of particular interest were people he met at those times. Having outlined his requirements, he informed her that she would be staying for the duration of her assignment at his home in West London. His wife Adele was expecting her that morning and would introduce her to a young detective constable seconded from Sussex Constabulary, one Helen Shaw. The two could then appear together as on a girls' night out, to avoid arousing suspicion in venues such as restaurants and pubs.

"You actually wish us both to enter such premises, whenever the suspect does so?" Janet Midler asked, taking to the idea.

"It will be an essential part of your duties," Mason explained. "The suspect always takes his evening meal out. He does not care for the hostel food. My senior, Bill Harrington, considers that an excellent opportunity to employ what is known as a roving bug."

The young woman's eyes opened wide.

"Which is what, exactly, Inspector?"

"It is quite straightforward," Mason replied. "On entering a pub or restaurant with your girlfriend, sit fairly near the suspect and surreptitiously place your cellphone beneath a table napkin. Do not switch it on, since if it rings during the course of a meal, it will attract attention."

"I get it," an intrigued sergeant replied. "We order a meal and engage in girl-talk about clothes, pop music, celebrities and the like."

"Exactly," Mason said, appreciating her grasp of the situation.

"You must ring Scotland Yard *before* you enter such premises. Our man there will shortly thereafter activate your cellphone microphone by remote control. The device will then pick up any conversations in its catchment area and transmit them to our listening post. Quite simple and straightforward."

"Modern technology is simply amazing," Janet Midler remarked.

"Isn't it so?" Mason agreed, sipping his Java coffee. "If you can do so unobserved, please also photograph any person the suspect happens to meet."

"I shall do my best, Inspector Mason," she assured him.

"Then good luck, Sergeant," he said. "I shall be away from London for a few days. I shall meet up with you at home on my return. Adele will take good care of you. On no account must you go to Scotland Yard."

"A fascinating assignment," Midler said. "Just my cup of tea."

"You will need this to recognize him," Mason then said, handing her a small photograph of his bogus protégé taken for official records.

"Quite good-looking," the young officer remarked, appraising it.

George Mason then gave directions on how to reach his home using the Underground and watched as she carried her small valise towards the escalator. He drained his coffee, which had gone quite cool, grabbed his suitcase and took the tube to Waterloo International, where he caught the mid-morning Eurostar service to Brussels. On arrival in the Belgian capital, he switched platforms and caught the express service to Cologne. It was mid-afternoon when he reached the Rhenish city, giving him a two-hour wait for his connection by Deutsche Bahn to Paderborn, from where he would take a local service to Bad Harzheim.

Having skipped lunch, he bought a grilled bratwurst lashed with mustard from a vendor on the station concourse, observing the to and fro of Kolner

Hauptbahnhof as he ate, before setting off to explore something of a city he had never previously visited. On emerging from the station, he followed the Rhine embankment, noting with interest the strong current and the large commercial barges heading against it on their way south towards Switzerland. The imposing lines of the storied cathedral soon caught his eye. Turning off the embankment, he followed Trunkgasse and entered the building through carved oaken doors. An official guide greeted him, pointing out features of particular interest. George Mason thanked her and strolled up the nave, admiring the stained-glass windows and the statuary. Set above the high altar was the Shrine of the Three Kings, a gilded reliquary said by the guide to contain the bones of the Magi, which found their way by a circuitous route to Cologne from Constantinople during the Middle Ages. Donating a few euros to the restauration fund on leaving, he marveled at the unexpected things one could come across in almost any part of Europe, it was so rich in history.

It was early evening by the time his local train arrived at Bad Harzheim. Direktor Weidman was there to meet him, having been notified by telephone from Cologne the likely time of his visitor's arrival.

"*Guten Abend, Inspektor,*" he greeted, as they shook hands.

"*Guten Abend, Herr Direktor,*" George Mason said, in his best German.

"Had a good trip?" Hans Weidman enquired.

"Excellent," Mason replied. "The cross-Channel rail service is a marvel, saving lots of time. I left

London around ten-thirty this morning, and here I am in central Germany."

"Good to have you here, Inspector," the other said, leading the way to his parked car.

The German officer then drove his visitor the short distance to Hotel Rheinfels, in the center of town, where accommodation had been pre-booked. He waited patiently in the foyer until Mason had checked in and deposited his luggage in his room, before inviting him to dinner at a Bad Harzheim restaurant serving local dishes. Over a tasty meal of schnitzels, helped down with a bottle of Moselle wine, the two men became well-acquainted. George Mason recounted his visit to Cologne Cathedral; while Hans Weidman recalled a visit to Westminster Abbey he had made years ago on a school trip.

*

The next morning, a junior officer arrived at the hotel immediately after breakfast to take the Scotland Yard officer to police headquarters. It was situated in a narrow, tree-lined alley the Germans call *gassen*. The director's office was on the ground floor at the rear of the building. He received his visitor cordially.

"*Guten Morgen, Herr Mason,*" he greeted. "*Haben Sie gut geschlaffen?*"

"I slept very well, thank you," Mason replied.

"Now, to serious business," the director began. "The situation, as I understand it, is that a certain individual managed to substitute himself for

Kommissar Brendt Schulz on the Europol exchange program."

"Quite amazingly," Mason replied, "that seems to be the case. The question is who."

"That is something we may soon establish," Hans Weidman said. "I contacted Hansa Lines at Hamburg immediately after your phone call from London. They faxed me the manifest of the *Bremerhaven* for the relevant trans-Atlantic voyage yesterday afternoon."

Saying that, he drew out a typed list from a desk folder and, adjusting his horn-rimmed spectacles, perused it carefully.

"You have withheld the discovery of Kommissar Schulz's body from the media, I take it, Herr Direktor?" his visitor asked.

"As a temporary measure, Inspector," the officer replied.

"It is crucial that the impostor does not get wind of it."

"I fully appreciate that, Herr Mason," the director assured him.

"What about the unfortunate man's family?" Mason asked.

"According to our records, he does not seem to have much in the way of family. He was an orphan, originally from Stuttgart. No next-of-kin is recorded on our personnel files."

"That solves one problem, at least," his visitor commented.

The director's gaze returned to the fax.

"Hansa Lines informed me that only a handful of cabins were booked for single occupancy on that particular date. The occupants included a clergyman, a member of the European Parliament, a schoolteacher traveling to Boston, a Frenchwoman headed to Cherbourg and another man, interestingly enough, who booked a passage to Southampton."

"Who might that be?" an alert George Mason asked.

"Somebody by the name of Otto Steiner."

"Any background on him?"

The German officer thought hard for a few moments.

"You know, Inspector, that name seems to ring a bell. I have a feeling I have come across it before."

He then keyed the name into his desk computer.

"He is listed here, incredibly, as a former member of the Hildesberg police!" he announced, within minutes.

"That might explain a lot," his visitor remarked, "if this is indeed our man. For one thing, it would explain his evident familiarity with police methods."

"He would also have had to know details of the Europol exchange program and the name of our chosen candidate."

"He is evidently somebody very close to you," Mason observed.

The polizei direktor shifted uncomfortably in his seat and gave Mason an almost agonized look.

"That would, unfortunately, seem to be the case," he ruefully admitted. "I shall put a call through to Hildesberg and see what they have to say."

With that, he picked up the phone and spoke for several minutes, tapping his fingers on his polished desk-top as he did so.

"Otto Steiner was dismissed from the Hildesberg force four years ago, for taking bribes," he informed his visitor. "He served a two-year term at Hannover Penitentiary and is suspected of being involved in rackets."

Kidnapping immediately suggested itself to George Mason.

"That might explain a lot, too," he remarked.

"Assuming that this is the same person as the individual you are currently hosting at the Metropolitan Police," Hans Weidman said, with heavy irony, "how do you propose to proceed, Inspector?"

"We shall need confirmation of his identity," George Mason replied. "I have already initiated surveillance of his activities outside of work. Where he goes, whom he meets, and so on. It should lead to some very interesting conclusions."

"The Hildesberg police are looking for leads on his activities," the German officer said. "Why don't we work together on this? I have a legitimate stake in this enquiry since Brendt Schulz was a valued member of our own department, operating out of this very office. I can coordinate our enquiries with the Hildesberg people, who will pick up the tab for any expenses you may incur."

George Mason judiciously nodded agreement.

"I think that would be very useful," he said.

At that moment, the telephone rang. The director picked up the receiver and listened attentively for a few moments.

"That was a call from Hansa Lines," he told his visitor. "The *Bremerhaven* is, by a stroke of luck, currently in dock at Hamburg. The shipping manager has interviewed crew members and he tells me that one of them noticed two youngish men smoking cigars on the upper deck after dinner. It was a very gusty night, he recalls. He saw no other passengers in the vicinity."

"Interesting circumstantial evidence," George Mason remarked.

At that point, coffee was served by a junior officer. Hans Weidman did the honors, pouring it into china cups.

"Cream and sugar?" he asked.

"A little cream, but no sugar," Mason replied, thinking of his waistline.

They partook of the small refreshment, which included slices of freshly-baked coffee cake, in silence for a few minutes. Steady rain began to spatter on the window-ledge, bringing a frown to the German's intelligent features.

"They are having a fete this afternoon at my daughter's school," he said. "Hope it clears up in time. You may come along if you wish, Inspector."

"I should be delighted," Mason said, ever keen to show an interest in the younger generation.

"We can have lunch together first at Wirtshaus zum Harzwald, an old staging inn on the way there. If you are a beer drinker, Herr Mason, they have an excellent selection on tap."

Such words were music to Mason's ears, since they also gave him an opportunity to extend his stay in this scenic part of Germany.

"I shall look forward to it," he said. "Thanks for the invitation."

"My pleasure," came the quick response. "After this meeting, you might take a quick look round our delightful town while I catch up with paperwork. Call back here around noon."

"Certainly," his visitor agreed. "But before I go, Herr Direktor, there is one other matter we need to discuss."

Hans Weidman nibbled at his coffee cake and returned a questioning look, while also checking the weather outside.

"Motive," George Mason said. "Assuming that this Otto Steiner is our suspect, which seems increasingly likely, what motive could he possibly have for tipping overboard from an ocean-going liner one of your own officers and taking his place on the Europol exchange program?"

"A very challenging question, indeed, Inspector Mason," the German officer said. "The ball, as you say in England, is now very much in your court on that issue."

George Mason returned a wry smile, drained his cup and left the office intent on exploring his new environment for the hour or so until noon. First, he would return to his hotel and place a call to his wife Adele, to enquire how the Birmingham officer was settling in.

*

Detective Sergeant Janet Midler, on taking leave of George Mason at Euston Station, took the Central Line tube to West Ruislip, arriving at the detective's home in a quiet cul-de-sac just before midday. Adele Mason greeted her cordially and showed her to the room allocated to her for the duration of her stay. After they had got to know each other a little over a light lunch of cold cuts and salad, Helen Shaw arrived by car from Sussex. Coming from the local police force at Haywards Heath, dealing mainly with routine day-to-day matters and the occasional serious crime, such as burglary and assault, she was quite excited at the prospect of joining a Scotland Yard investigation. Janet Midler explained the concept of a roving bug, a procedure that only increased the young constable's sense of anticipation.

Shortly after their arrival, Chief Inspector Harrington faxed though to the Mason home the bogus kommissar's schedule for the week ahead, keeping everything as apparently normal routine. He would clock off that day at 4.00 p.m. The two young detectives left West Ruislip at three o'clock, taking the tube to Oxford Circus, where they switched to the Bakerloo Line. On regaining street-level at Maida Vale, they entered a coffee bar across the street from the police hostel to await developments. Several young police cadets entered or left the building, until at around 4.30 p.m. Janet Midler spotted an older person resembling the photograph George Mason had given her. She observed him enter the hostel and re-emerge twenty minutes later, heading up the main street. The two women quit the coffee bar and followed him at a discreet distance. He visited a tobacconist and a bookshop, remaining inside for fifteen minutes before retracing his steps past the hostel to enter the local sauna.

"We can hardly follow him in there," Helen Shaw remarked.

"Unfortunately not," Janet Midler replied. "Inspector Mason is mainly concerned about whom he meets. A sauna would be as good a place as any for a secretive rendezvous."

"Pity it isn't a mixed sauna," her companion humorously observed, as the two detectives bided their time browsing in a nearby garment store.

About an hour later, the German re-emerged into the daylight, walking directly towards the Underground station. They followed him as he took the tube to Oxford Circus, where he switched to the Central Line as far as Holland Park. On re-surfacing, he covered the short distance to a pub named the Bird in Hand, situated on the far side of the village green, pausing to smoke a cigarette before entering. Detective Sergeant Midler then alerted Scotland Yard to activate the roving bug, before she and Helen Shaw entered the pub together and occupied a table close to where their target was sitting. Janet Midler crossed to the bar to order two glasses of Chardonnay, noting as she did so a second man with a vaguely foreign aspect enter the pub lounge and join the bogus kommissar at table, where they wasted no time in perusing the evening menu.

The detective sergeant regained her seat, withdrew her cell phone and placed it beneath a table napkin, as George Mason had instructed. It was now turned six o'clock and it seemed apparent to the two detectives that they could be there for the best part of the evening. The Bird in Hand soon began to fill with regular patrons hanging round the bar area or occupying spare tables, so that the detectives' presence there did not in any way stand out. Janet Midler, concerned that the television broadcast might drown out the bug, requested the barman to turn the volume down. He adjusted it just a little, before taking their order for food. It proved to be a typical girls' night out, as the two women tackled vegetable quiche with French fries and got to know each other, finding things in common while discussing boyfriends, clothes and aspects of their careers in the police.

On finishing their steak-and-kidney pie, the two men ordered more beer and became engrossed in conversation, seemingly oblivious of the general ambience of the pub. At nine o'clock, they suddenly rose from their places and quickly left the premises. Janet Midler decided not to follow. She had already achieved her objective for that day, she decided, and did not wish to risk being noticed by the German, who seemed very alert to his surroundings, with an eye for attractive women. She decided to stay put for the next ten minutes, allowing Helen Shaw time to finish her third glass of wine. They then left the Bird in Hand together and took the tube back to West Ruislip, arriving there a little after ten o'clock. Adele Mason kindly made them tea before they retired.

For the next two days, the seconded detectives followed a similar routine. On the Tuesday, their target did not emerge from the police hostel until turned six o'clock. He ate alone at a local pizzeria before entering the Odeon cinema, where an American romantic comedy was playing. That put Janet Midler and her companion in a bind. They had already seen the film and saw little point in spending two hours inside a cinema, where the roving bug would only transmit film dialogue to the listening post at Scotland Yard. They decided to call it a day, returning to West Ruislip to watch television for the remainder of the evening. In the absence of her husband, Adele Mason was pleased to have their company. Since the two detectives had not eaten, she ordered Chinese take-aways for them.

The following day proved more interesting. The bogus kommissar left the hostel at five o'clock and took the tube to Charing Cross, where he met up with a young blonde woman dressed for the warm evening in a skirt and blouse. The two detectives followed them down to the Thames Embankment, where they strolled for an hour, pausing from time to time to observe the tourist launches and the barges on the busy river. On leaving the riverside, the couple walked back to Fleet Street and entered a pub called The Cheshire Cheese for their evening meal. Janet Midler and Helen Shaw followed suit, occupying a table within earshot of the romantic couple. Since they were by now quite hungry after a longish walk, they ordered lamb cutlets with baked potato, helped down by a half-carafe of Valpollicela. Janet Midler discreetly placed her cell phone beneath the table napkin, having alerted the listening post before entering the premises. It was an even livelier venue than the Bird in Hand, being a favorite haunt of journalists from nearby newspaper offices. On finishing their meal, the couple quickly rose from table, left the pub and walked at a brisk pace along Fleet Street towards The Strand.

The detectives tailed them as they took the tube as far as Swiss Cottage on the Jubilee Line. Once there, the couple walked arm-in-arm a short distance along the main street, before taking a left turn to enter a modern apartment building. Janet Midler and Helen Shaw walked past it unobserved, noting the name of the street. They then re-crossed the main street a little farther ahead and strolled back to the Underground station, aware that there was little they could now achieve at Swiss Cottage. It was almost nine o'clock by this time; time to call it a day as far as detective work was concerned. The young Sussex constable wished to see the lights in the West End theater district, so they took the tube to Piccadilly Circus, mixed with the crowd for a while and entered a disco to fill out the evening.

"It seems that our target has made a romantic conquest," Janet Midler remarked.

"And why not?" came the reply. "He is quite a good-looking guy. Do you happen to know why we are tailing him?"

The sergeant shook her head.

"It is all very hush-hush," she said. "Our brief is to follow orders and not ask questions."

...

Chapter Nine

On arrival back at Scotland Yard on Thursday, George Mason reported to Bill Harrington. The chief inspector was in buoyant mood, owing to the successful employment of the roving bug by officers Midler and Shaw. First, he had some news to convey.

"Yesterday, Walter Stopford sent me the results of the lab tests he conducted at your request," he said. "Ian MacQuarrie has been cleared of any involvement in the death of Rainer Weiss."

"His DNA does not match the sample on the sauropod rib?" Mason asked.

The chief inspector shook his head.

"We are back to square one," he remarked. "I rang the professor at Lothian University immediately on getting the result. He was very relieved."

"I imagine so," Mason observed, "since there were significant grounds for suspecting him."

"Our German friend's pet theory, for what it was worth."

"Where is the impostor right now?"

"Inspector Greenhalgh has him well in hand, doing more routine work. He seemed put out at being removed from the Weiss case, but he does not suspect the reason. I told him the results of the lab test, which he could hardly challenge. We are making everything seem as normal as possible in our dealings with him."

"He considers that you are just varying the menu a bit?"

"Exactly, Inspector. Now how did you fare at Bad Harzheim?"

"Quite successfully," George Mason replied. "I met with the police director, Hans Weidman, who had been in touch with Hansa Lines regarding the manifest of the *Bremerhaven*. He proposed a certain Otto Steiner, an ex-cop as it happens, as the likely suspect. Steiner is also suspected of involvement in various rackets. Weidman wants us to coordinate our efforts to shed light on these. He is concerned that a corrupt ex-cop may have contacts actively serving with the Hildesberg police. They do not want any rot to spread and will underwrite any expenses we may incur in the course of our enquiries."

Bill Harrington listened carefully to what his subordinate had to say, his face breaking into a rare broad smile. He leaned forward in his chair and said:

"By Jove, Inspector, that is it! You have hit the nail on the head!"

A bemused George Mason returned a questioning look.

"There is an Otto recorded by the roving bug," Harrington explained, "conversing with an individual by the name of Oleg. Detective Sergeant Midler eavesdropped on them at a pub called the Bird in Hand at Holland Park."

It was Mason's turn to register a broad smile.

"Oleg is a person of much interest in this investigation," he remarked. "Alison Aubrey has already tied him to Fletchers school and to the Darwinian Institute."

"So the two are in cahoots?"

"It would appear so, Chief Inspector," Mason said. "Play me the recording of the transmission from Holland Park."

"By all means," Harrington replied. "There is quite a lot of background noise, I am afraid, what with the pub regulars and the television, that has drowned out some of the conversation. But I think you will get the gist of things. It seems mainly to be about wine. Dinard was mentioned."

The senior man then requested coffee service, which Alison Aubrey provided within minutes, before the two officers settled down to listening to what was salvaged from a conversation in a lively pub. Afterwards, just before noon, George Mason said:

"They seem very keen on soccer, Chief Inspector."

"They both seem enthusiastic fans of teams in the German Bundesliga."

"Otto talks a lot about a girl named Rita, too," Mason remarked.

"Janet Midler told me that on Tuesday evening he met a girl at Charing Cross, with whom he spent part of the evening at The Cheshire Cheese on Fleet Street, before heading to what Midler assumed was the girl's apartment at Swiss Cottage. The bug was also employed at the pub, but the background noise overwhelmed it. The place is a favorite watering-hole of Fleet Street journalists, who usually have plenty to say about anything and everything."

"Those two girls did a great job," Mason said. "We shall retain their services for the rest of this week, then replace them with personnel from the Middlesex force, to avoid arousing any suspicion on Steiner's part. We shall probably use a man and a woman, to appear as a couple."

"Good thinking, Inspector," Bill Harrington said. "He could possibly recognize two attractive females if they showed up too often at his regular haunts. Now, as far as I understand this recording, Otto Steiner has instructed the other individual, named Oleg, to pay a visit to an establishment called Vins du Midi at Dinard."

"Steiner is evidently the main player in this curious duo," his colleague said. "Vins du Midi sounds like the name of a wine merchant. Dinard is a popular resort on the coast of Brittany."

"Across the bay from St. Malo, I believe," Harrington said. "Went there decades ago with my wife, not long after we were married."

"It used to be the top seaside resort in France," Mason said, "until Riviera resorts such as Cannes, St. Tropez and Antibes overtook it."

"So you will have an interesting trip, Inspector."

George Mason returned a look of pleasant surprise.

"You are asking me to go to Dinard?" he asked.

"We need to find out what they are up to, Inspector. On this recording, as far as I can make out, Oleg is also being told to transfer the money to a bank. But it does not say which bank."

"At a guess, Chief Inspector," Mason said, "it would likely be a bank in Switzerland or Luxembourg."

"Let us put two and two together," Harrington then said, with an artful grin, "and see if we can make five. Otto Steiner and this Oleg character are either operating a protection racket or they have some sort of stake in the wine business, which may or may not be legitimate."

George Mason returned an ironic look.

"I would not place any bets on its legitimacy," he said.

"Since we have no idea of Oleg's itinerary or timetable," Harrington then said, "I should like you to visit the wine merchant yourself, as a potential customer, and find out what you can. You have a good nose for shady dealings. Leave first thing Monday morning. You could be there and back in a day."

*

After a relaxing weekend, George Mason rose at five o'clock on the Monday morning. Without disturbing his wife's rest, he shaved and dressed, skipped breakfast and caught the tube to Paddington Station. He was in good time for the 7.09 a.m. express service to Southampton. On arrival there, he took a taxi to the port and boarded the early-morning ferry to Dinard. It was a fine day in late spring, allowing him the opportunity to stroll the deck as the boat headed down The Solent towards the English

Channel. After a while, he repaired to the cafeteria for a late breakfast of smoked haddock, toast and strong coffee. His fellow passengers were, he decided, mainly tourists heading out to the Emerald Coast for an early-season vacation. In common with Bill Harrington, he was fairly familiar with the terrain, having spent a motoring holiday touring Brittany with Adele some years ago. They had rounded off their trip with a visit to Normandy, mainly to see the off-shore abbey-fortress of Mont St. Michel, which featured strongly in medieval wars against the English.

When the boat docked around mid-morning, he proceeded along the promenade towards Place General de Gaulle, a spacious square bordered by colorful flower beds. He soon located the tourist office in a side-street off the square, obtaining directions to Vins du Midi. On reaching the merchant's premises, a large double-fronted emporium on Rue Foch, he entered tentatively and moved slowly down the aisles examining the labels on the bottles.

"*Je peux vous aider?*" the owner politely enquired, after serving a customer.

"*Peut-etre,*" the detective replied, in his best French. "Maybe."

"We have the premier selection of wines in Brittany," the man then said. "They are very popular with our visitors."

"I am looking for something special," George Mason said.

"Our top-quality merchandise, Monsieur? Please to step this way."

He led the way to a small room at the rear of the building and stood discreetly in the background while his visitor examined the stock. After several minutes so doing, the detective turned to the proprietor and said:

"You have some interesting rare wines, Monsieur. Chateau Ronsard 1891, for example. And Caves de Montserrat 1850."

"They are among our top lines," the Frenchman agreed.

"I may well be interested in making a purchase," George Mason then said. "If that is the case, I shall call back presently."

He then left the premises and located the nearest post office, known in France as the P.T.T., and placed a telephone call to London.

"Inspector Mason!" came the voice of the chief inspector. "Good to hear from you. How are things progressing?"

"I just called at Vins du Midi," George Mason said. "I have never seen such pricey wines in my entire life."

"Tempted to buy, Inspector?"

"I thought it might be useful to sample some of their wares," came the reply. "It seems a legitimate enough business on the surface, but Otto Steiner's connection with it obviously raises questions. I need cash at short notice."

"How much?" Harrington warily enquired.

"About five thousand euros."

There was an audible gasp over the line.

"You cannot be serious, Inspector," Harrington boomed. "Where do we find that kind of money?"

"It will be just a temporary loan," Mason assured him. "Direktor Weidman told me that the Hildesberg police will cover all expenses."

The senior man weighed up the situation.

"I could arrange a wire transfer," he said, "from our special purposes account at Westminster Bank. The superintendent need not know about it, if your German friends refund it within days."

"Have it wired it to Banque de Bretagne, Rue Jules Verne," Mason said.

"Will do, Inspector. I sincerely hope you know what you are doing. Since when, for instance, were you a connoisseur of fine wines?"

George Mason smiled to himself at that remark.

"One reads things," he replied, "in the Sunday magazines, for example."

"A lot of baloney, in my opinion. At blind tastings, even experts can often not tell the difference between rare wines and *vin ordinaire*."

"If you say so, Chief Inspector. I shall call at the bank here in about an hour's time, collect the funds and purchase some bottles. I should be able to catch the four o'clock sailing back to Southampton."

"I shall be very interested to-morrow morning to see what you have spent our money on," Harrington gruffly replied, before ringing off.

George Mason left the post office and took a stroll round the main shopping area of Dinard, calling at a bookstore to pass the time. They stocked large volumes of reproductions of paintings by such as van Gogh, Pissaro and Seurat, which he took much pleasure in browsing, before buying a French novel to read on the trip back to Southampton. It being now midday, he left the store and located a sidewalk café on Rue Jules Verne, a few blocks from the bank, where he ordered quiche Lorraine for lunch, followed by Rocquefort cheese and crackers. It pleased him hugely to dine outdoors and observe the pedestrian traffic in this most attractive resort town. The food was good and the weather fine. Feeling no great sense of urgency, he eventually made his way back to the bank, collected the wire transfer and revisited Vins du Midi, where he purchased, to the owner's evident satisfaction, six bottles of rare wine.

On reaching home that evening, he met with Detective Sergeant Ron Fielding and Detective Constable June Aldrich, from the Middlesex Constabulary; they had been assigned to replace Janet Midler and Helen Shaw for surveillance purposes. He explained to them the nature of the operation, told them how to use the roving bug and handed them photographs of the suspects that Sergeant Midler had managed to take with her cellphone, along with Otto Steiner's schedule.

"Since your base is Greater London," he said, "you will easily reach Maida Vale by tube. Directly opposite the police hostel there is a coffee bar called The Daily Grind. From there you can observe all comings and goings across the way. Any questions?"

"What about those occasions when we cannot tail the suspect?" Ron Fielding asked.

"You will just have to call it a day," George Mason replied. "Last week, for example, the suspect met with a girlfriend at Charing Cross, winding up after a meal at The Cheshire Cheese at her apartment at Swiss Cottage. Several times a week, he frequents the Bird in Hand pub at Holland Park. That is where you will best employ your cellphone. Remember to alert Scotland Yard beforehand."

"What type of clothing should we wear, Inspector?" Constable Aldrich asked.

"Casual clothes," came the reply. "Act like a courting couple, if possible."

Ron Fielding turned towards his colleague, an attractive brunette, with a mischievous grin.

"That should not present any problem," he said.

June Aldrich dug him in the ribs with her elbow for that remark, while giving a rather coquettish smile.

After the two new recruits had returned to their Middlesex homes, George Mason showed Adele the wines he had purchased at Dinard. She was very impressed, handling each bottle delicately while figuring out the French labels.

"I never imagined you were so knowledgeable about wine," she said, admiringly.

Her husband returned an ironic look.

"I am not, particularly," he admitted. "I just went for the priciest."

The pair then settled down to a late dinner of Swiss steak, helped down with a bottle of *vin ordinaire*.

*

The next day, George Mason reported to Bill Harrington immediately on arrival at the office.

"Had a good trip, Inspector?" his senior cordially asked.

"You bet, Chief Inspector. I bought six examples of the best stock from Vins du Midi," Mason informed him.

"So where is this priceless plonk?"

"In my car trunk. I chose not to bring them inside, for fear of alerting our German friend."

"You need have no worries on that score," the other remarked. "Our friend Otto is on an assignment with Roy Greenhalgh. A case of suspected fraud at a bank in Chelsea. They will be there most of the morning, at least."

"I could bring the wines up, if you wish."

"No real need," Harrington replied. "I am not really a wine buff. Malt whisky is more my line."

That was hardly news to George Mason.

"What you can now do," the senior man continued, "is establish their authenticity. But first, get on the phone to Bad Harzheim and request repayment of our investment from your friend Hans Weidman."

George Mason promised to do that.

"What procedure do we adopt for the wines?" he tentatively asked.

"We shall require an expert, obviously," Harrington replied, with a hint of sarcasm. "I have found the man you need, in fact. While you were sunning yourself on the Emerald Coast, I looked into the matter. There is an oenologist named Pierre Pelletier based at Covent Garden. He is an acknowledged authority on French wines. Go over there this morning, after you have rung Bad Harzheim. Now, if you will excuse me, Inspector, I have a meeting with the superintendent."

"May I ask you one question before I leave?" George Mason said.

"By all means. Fire away."

"How did you learn about using a roving bug, Chief Inspector?"

"From the F.B.I.," came the quick reply. "They demonstrated it to me when I went over last year to study American police methods."

"How come we haven't used it before?"

"The opportunity did not arise….until now, Inspector."

"Very useful it is, too. Without such a device, we might have struggled to crack this case."

"I thought you might find you it helpful, Inspector," Bill Harrington genially replied.

George Mason returned to his own office and placed a call to Germany. Direktor Weidman was only too pleased to refund the five thousand euros, being much intrigued at the English detective's line of enquiry. Mason then gave him account details for the wire transfer to Westminster Bank.

"I shall be very interested to hear, Inspector," Weidman said, "if the wines are genuine or not."

"I should be able to get back to you later today," George Mason said, politely enquiring about his counterpart's family before ringing off.

On checking the small backlog of mail accumulated during his short absence, he exchanged the time of day with Alison Aubrey and quit the office to retrieve his car from the underground parking area. The rush-hour traffic had subsided by now, giving him a quick drive to Covent Garden. He parked his vehicle and located Pierre Pelletier's premises in a narrow street running behind the celebrated opera house. The wine expert was pleasantly surprised to receive a visitor from Scotland Yard, inviting him into his cluttered office.

"What can I do for you, Inspector?" he enquired in heavily-accented English, while offering his visitor a seat.

The detective quickly scanned the room, which was lined with shelves holding tomes seemingly about every wine-producing country round the globe. The walnut desk held a stack of brochures, promotional leaflets and travel guides, including a European Rail Timetable, convincing the visitor that the oenologist traveled quite a lot in his line of work. A box of Cuban cigars held pride of place and a faint aroma of tobacco lingered in the air.

"I was recommended to you, Monsieur Pelletier," Mason said, "as a leading expert on French wines. I am particularly concerned about wine fraud."

The Frenchman coughed and cleared his throat.

"That, Inspector, is a regrettable aspect of our trade," he said, with a frown. "It may take several forms."

"Such as?" Mason prompted.

"As concerns reds, the darker the color, the better the wine, in general terms. Naturally occurring phenols in the grapes themselves affect color, but additives such as elderberry juice may be used to deepen it, in the same way that cinnamon or ginger may be added to improve the flavor."

"Remarkable," the detective said. "But at least they are not harmful additives. I seem to recall more hazardous substances being sometimes used in wine-making."

Pierre Pelletier, a rotund figure with wisps of blond hair over a balding pate, gravely shook his head.

"That practice, fortunately, is very rare," he replied. "You are referring, for example, to adding methanol, a toxic form of wood alcohol. It is a criminal offence."

"I believe that the Finns distill wood alcohol in the pine forests," his visitor remarked. "They call it jaloviina."

"They are welcome to it, Inspector," Pelletier observed, with a look of distaste. "Prolonged consumption, however, may seriously affect one's sight."

"Perhaps they do it to bypass the state monopoly on liquor."

"The alcohol policy in those northern countries is rather strict, as I understand it," the Frenchman observed. "It may be the winter darkness that induces people to drink heavily. Hence the state endeavors to control all liquor sales."

"You mentioned coloring and flavoring of wines," the detective said. "Anything else?"

"A vintner may purchase cheaper wines and blend them with his own product, to expand his output. That was quite a common practice in former times, for example to produce sufficient quantities of claret for the English market. But the most significant wine fraud today, in my view, concerns labeling."

"Can you enlarge on that, Monsieur Pelletier?"

"There have been some notable scams in recent years," the expert said, "mainly in the market for rare wines and at wine auctions. The conman creates a fake label for a regular bottle of wine and sells it as a rare vintage. The fraud is so convincing that wine aficionados and collectors are often taken in."

"That is truly amazing," the detective remarked.

"The trouble is, Inspector, that the deception may only come to light when the bottle is opened, which may be several years after it is purchased. Even then, the victim may not detect the fraud."

"I have some rare wines with me," his visitor then said. "Would you be able to tell me whether they are genuine or not?"

"In so far as I am able, certainly," came the reply. "But it may involve uncorking them."

"No problem," Mason said, leaving the office to retrieve the samples from his car trunk.

On his return, he produced the six bottles from a small plaid hold-all and stood them upright on the office desk. Pierre Pelletier eyed them with great interest.

"You have quite a selection here," he said, much intrigued. "Where did you acquire them?"

"That is something I prefer not to disclose at the moment," the detective said, "since this wine is part of an ongoing criminal investigation."

"I understand perfectly," the other said, holding up one of the bottles and reading the label out loud. "Chateau Ronsard 1891."

He peered skeptically at it, put it down and crossed to a bookshelf, from where he took down a large volume on Burgundy estate wines.

"I have never come across a Chateau Ronsard," he said, quickly consulting the index at the back of the tome. "In fact, it is not listed here. It is quite evidently a fake."

George Mason felt inwardly gratified that his efforts had not been in vain, as Pierre Pelletier examined a second bottle.

"Caves de Montserrat 1850," he read. "That is a genuine label, Inspector. I have dealt with it many times over the years. The vintner is very reliable and of excellent reputation. This wine would not be blended or adulterated in any way."

"Fair enough," the detective said.

"Now what do we have next?" the other asked, examining a third bottle. "Garonne le Duc 1902. An interesting Bordeaux estate, Inspector, that has been implicated from time to time in blending its products with cheaper Italian vintages."

He placed it on one side and examined the three remaining bottles in turn, pronouncing the last of them as another instance of fake labeling, since it was not listed in the catalog of Rhone wines. Replacing the tomes on their shelves, he proceeded to uncork the bottle he had set aside, while his visitor looked on with keen interest. He then poured a small measure into a glass and sampled it.

"This is a blend," he pronounced, "but a very good one. Care to try it?"

"Don't mind if I do," replied the intrigued detective, who had never in his life paid more than a few pounds for a bottle of wine.

Pelletier poured him a fairly generous measure, while recharging his own glass.

"*Bon sante,*" he said.

"*Sante,*" Mason rejoined, in his best French. "Your good health."

"What do you propose to do with these wines?" the expert then asked, as they stood together by the office window enjoying a convivial moment together.

"I shall use them as evidence," Mason replied.

"But you have three genuine bottles, Inspector. I would make you an offer for them. I am employed most evenings as a sommelier at a hotel in Mayfair. I can always use good wines."

George Mason could only smile at that request.

"I would have to check beforehand with the purchaser," he replied, setting his glass back on the desk, while secretly hoping that Direktor Weidman would allow him to retain the genuine ones. The suspect bottles would be needed as evidence in any upcoming court case.

Chapter Ten

Ilsa Weiss woke early in her home in the upmarket suburb of Unterwalden. She showered and partially dressed before preparing a substantial breakfast for the busy day ahead. After a leisurely meal, she finished dressing, fixed her hair and slipped out of the house. Minutes later, she was driving her Audi towards the center of Hildesberg, pleased to note that the sky was clearing after overnight rain. On parking her car, she entered the headquarters of Freiheit Partei, where she was greeted by her campaign manager Werner Hess and a small group of well-wishers who had voluntarily assisted in the run-up to the state election by making telephone calls and door-to-door visits to prospective voters in the city and adjoining suburbs. The candidate thanked them for their efforts on her behalf and mingled with them as they partook of the coffee and freshly-baked croissants provided for them.

Less than an hour later, at just turned ten-thirty, she left with Werner Hess to cover on foot the short distance to the Stadthaus. On arrival, she was met by representatives of the media, reporters, press photographers and TV cameramen crowding the entrance. She elbowed through, skillfully evading questions about her election prospects while presenting a cheerful, upbeat image to the cameras before entering the polling station to cast her vote. Her campaign manager fended off the more persistent paparazzi and followed suit. The booths had opened at 7 a.m. According to officials, business had been steady all morning and was expected to grow brisker by late-afternoon, as people left their place of work. Feeling satisfied with the good turn-out, Ilsa and Werner left the building and walked back to their office. The campaign volunteers had by now dispersed, leaving the candidate and her manager to their own company.

"The good turn-out will help your candidacy," Werner Hess remarked, pouring generous measures of schnapps to mark the occasion.

"I sincerely hope so," Ilsa Weiss replied. "The Greens and the Social Democrats both have strong candidates"

"But they do not have your background in public service," her manager said. "Your work for the Ordnungs Kommission will carry weight with the general public, especially since I got *Hildesberg Abendblatt* to do an article on the decrease in violent crime over the past twelve months."

Ilsa sipped her schnapps while reviewing the situation.

"Good thinking, Werner," she remarked. "And our financial position is strong."

"We have comfortably outspent our opponents," Hess replied.

"Thanks, in no small part, to our key backers, Werner. Donations from the general public, on the other hand, were somewhat disappointing. Below expectations."

"That would be explained," her manager rejoined, "by the economic situation and the stagnation in wages. Money is tight these days. There is a movement afoot to get the federal government to provide more stimulus to the economy."

"Which may be all very well in the long run," Ilsa wryly remarked, "after years of belt-tightening across the euro-zone."

Werner Hess went to refill their glasses at the mini-bar.

"You may also benefit from the sympathy vote," he suggested, on regaining his seat.

"The death of my husband?" she enquired, with a touch of irony.

"Professor Weiss was a well-known figure throughout the state, particularly in this city. His unfortunate demise and the circumstances surrounding it will resonate with the general public. I estimate it will mean at least three percentage points in your favor."

"You may, or may not, be right," Ilsa replied. "I would not personally overestimate the finer feelings of voters. They act on issues that closely affect themselves. Quite hard-boiled in that respect. As for Rainer, his reputation rested mainly on the high-profile disputes he engaged in, not only on home ground, but also apparently during his tenure at Wessex University."

Werner Hess returned a wry smile at the last remark.

"I was not aware of that," he said, rather sheepishly.

"Oh, he was in the thick of things over in England, all right. Something about a new species of hominid discovered in northern Scotland."

"I read about that somewhere," the other remarked. "Perhaps in one of our dailies."

"*Homo caledoniensis*, they are calling it, Caledonia being the Roman name for Scotland."

"A fascinating subject, paleontology."

"I do not need reminding of that," came the tart response.

After savoring his schnapps in silence for a while, the campaign manager said:

"In any event, we shall have the results by tomorrow morning, when I fully expect you shall be named as the new president of North Saxony."

"I shall drink to that," she promptly replied, raising her glass.

*

In the evening of that same day, as the Masons were relaxing in front of the television set with a glass of Caves de Montserrat 1850 – Hans Weidman had generously offered them one of the genuine bottles, while reserving the others for a Germany Embassy function – they received a telephone call from the chief inspector.

"Good evening, Inspector," Harrington said. "I apologize for the late call, but I just received some interesting information via the roving bug at the Bird in Hand, Holland Park. Thought I should pass it on without delay."

"No problem, Chief Inspector," George Mason replied. "My wife and I are just enjoying a glass of wine while watching the news on television." He refrained from mentioning Weidman's gift, for fear of irking his senior. It was indeed very palatable wine, dark and smooth as velvet.

"Fielding and Aldrich managed to occupy a table quite near the suspects, without arousing suspicion. The cellphone transmission gives us another good lead."

"I am pleased to hear that," Mason said. "I felt sure the Middlesex officers could act the loving couple quite successfully."

"So it would seem," Harrington remarked. "Now get this, Mason. The individual named Oleg will be traveling to Zurich the day after tomorrow. He will take the Eurostar to Paris, where he will switch trains to Zurich. He has booked into Hotel Storchen."

"That is a five-star hotel," George Mason recalled, from previous visits to the city, "overlooking the River Limmat."

"Living it up on the proceeds of his wine dealings, eh?"

"More than likely, Chief Inspector. Pierre Pelletier questioned three of the bottles I obtained at Dinard. I am reserving them as possible evidence in any criminal proceedings."

"What about the genuine ones?" Harrington was quick to enquire.

"I conferred with Hans Weidman about those," Mason replied. "Since his department paid for them, he is reserving them for their London embassy. I intend to deliver them there first thing tomorrow."

"Make sure you don't open any, Inspector," the other half-seriously quipped. "I am aware of your predilection for fine wines."

"Chief Inspector!" George Mason remonstrated. "Would I do such a thing?"

The senior officer ignored the rhetorical question and said:

"You are to go to Zurich and book into Hotel Storchen ahead of the suspect's arrival. Take an afternoon flight from Gatwick. Sergeant Aubrey will accompany you, so that you can alternate the surveillance routine, to avoid arousing his suspicion."

"That should work very well," Mason said. "Alison has assisted me on several foreign assignments, very capably too."

"Call at my office tomorrow after your visit to the German Embassy. I have a fairly clear photograph of Oleg that Janet Midler managed to take at the Bird in Hand, to help you identify your quarry."

"Will do, Chief Inspector," his colleague said, replacing the receiver and rejoining Adele.

*

Two days later, the two detectives arrived at Kloten Airport in the early evening and took the rail link to Zurich Hauptbahnhof. Once there, George Mason checked the arrival times of trains from Paris. There were, in fact, only two inter-city services. The overnight one left from Gare de l'Est at 11 p.m.; the day service left from Gare d'Austerlitz at 2.15 p.m. The pair then walked a short distance along the Limmat embankment until they reached the waterside hotel, crowned by a large bronze effigy of a stork. After checking in, they freshened up in their respective rooms and met up again within the hour. Estimating that Oleg Volkov would reach the Storchen at around nine o'clock, they decided to spend the early part of the evening over dinner.

With that object in mind, they continued along the embankment to the point where the Limmat emerged from Lake Zurich, where they entered a beer garden that Mason had frequented on earlier visits to the city. The attraction, to his mind, was the al fresco dining, with views across the lake towards the snow-capped alps; not to mention the traditional Swiss fare. A quartet played popular music, mixed with traditional jazz, for the younger couples to dance to, most of the clientele being middle-aged or retired tourists perhaps less-inclined to shake a leg after a day's sightseeing. At the self-service counter, the detectives chose bratwurst with roesti and steins of the local Hurlimann's beer, finding a table so situated that they could observe the river traffic of tourist launches and six-man rowing crews from the various colleges located in the city. Alison Aubrey thought they might be in training for a regatta.

Her colleague was pleased to note that she enjoyed both the food and the ambience of his chosen venue, which was a novel experience for her. He was also aware that she was not completely up-to-date with developments in the case, following Bill Harrington's decision to keep things as tight as possible, to avoid alerting the German interloper. As far as Alison knew, Oleg Volkov was the only person of interest at this stage. She had no suspicions whatsoever regarding Otto Steiner, whom she continued to treat as a legitimate Europol exchange officer.

"What I should like you to do tomorrow," he said, as they rounded off their meal with coffee and apple strudel, "is follow the suspect from the moment he leaves the hotel and report back to me the places he visits."

"I can certainly do that, George," Alison assured him, a little surprised at her solo mission. "This place is full of tourists, so I will hardly stand out from the crowd. But what will you be doing meanwhile?"

"I intend to pay a visit to the Polizei Dienst," he informed her, "to renew contact with an old associate of mine, Leutnant Rudi Kubler. We worked together on a criminal investigation a few years back."

"A case you undoubtedly managed to crack," the young officer said, buttering his ego.

"We certainly did," he replied, with a broad smile.

They listened awhile to the musicians, who had switched to jazz. The sun began to set, casting a reddish glow over the lake, as the beer garden attracted more of the younger element, mainly for drinking and dancing.

"When we get back to England," George Mason suddenly said, "I should like you to invite the kommissar to your home for the day. A Saturday or Sunday would be fine. It does not matter which."

Alison thought that was an appealing idea.

"I would love to," she said. "It is time we showed him some genuine English hospitality, now that he has been with us for a while. A barbecue should work well. Malcolm loves doing them and he is a dab hand."

"That is settled then," a gratified George Mason said, without telling her the reason for his request, which had very little bearing on hospitality.

As dusk descended, they quit the beer garden and strolled back to the hotel, just in time to observe Oleg Volkov check in at the reception desk and go straight up to his room.

"We should order room service for breakfast," Mason said, "to preserve our cover. When you come downstairs afterwards, Alison, take up a position in the main lounge. They will have a selection of English-language magazines for visitors, which you can skim through while keeping an eye on the comings and goings in the dining area."

The next day, Alison Aubrey took an early breakfast and went down to the hotel lounge, as her senior had instructed. She found a back number of *Cosmopolitan* to flick through, while occupying an armchair with a good view of the dining-room, where a warm buffet was in progress. At just turned eight-thirty, her quarry made his entrance, remaining inside a mere thirty minutes before heading out into the street. The detective sergeant followed him at a safe distance, as he crossed Munsterplatz and headed towards the Altstadt, with its maze of steep, cobbled alleys the Swiss call *gassen*. He then suddenly entered a doorway part-way up a long flight of stone steps. Alison was almost out of breath as she climbed past the premises, noting with an inward groan that it was a men's sauna. Since she could hardly follow him inside, she proceeded to the top of the steps to reach the Lindenhof, a small tree-fringed park with a panoramic view of the city. In bright morning sunshine, she sat down on a bench affording a good view of the sauna entrance and contented herself with listening to a student violinist perform what she took to be a Bach sonata.

One hour later, Oleg Volkov emerged and quickly retraced his steps through the old quarter until he reached the river bank. The young detective almost lost him in the twists and turns of the narrow alleys and finally spotted him proceeding along a covered boardwalk, where he entered a jewelry store set amid a row of boutiques featuring wood crafts, glassware, rare prints and maps, Russian icons, fashion accessories and a perfumery. What a fascinating place Zurich was, she mused, noting the name EBNOTHER over the lintel of the jewelry store, as she took in the various window displays. An icon would suit her mother, who liked religious artifacts, but the price-tags were prohibitive.

When her quarry eventually left Ebnother's carrying a large package, she followed him as he crossed the Water Bridge to reach the Limmatquai on the opposite bank. He then walked briskly in the direction of the lake, crossing the busy intersection called Belle Vue and continuing past the Opera House along Seefeldstrasse. Alison then saw him enter a large stone-fronted building with a brass name-plate outside that read MARCUS BEHRENS. She walked past the building, crossed the busy street and stationed herself on a wooden bench in a small park bordered by flower-beds, noting that several species, like the wegelia, bloomed earlier here than in England. She had a good view of the building opposite, even if it was occasionally obscured by passing trams.

Twenty minutes later, Oleg Volkov left the premises and headed back towards the center of the city. She tailed him at a discreet distance, convinced that he had not noticed her, as he proceeded past the garden restaurant she had visited last evening and the Stadthaus, the city's administrative headquarters. On reaching Bahnhofstrasse, the main thoroughfare, he followed it until it issued in the Bahnhofplatz, which he crossed to enter the main station. Once there, he bought coffee and a newspaper, remaining at the catering stand for twenty minutes before crossing the station concourse towards the ticket booths. The young detective lingered by a bookstore, examining the titles on the racks outside. She watched him buy a ticket and proceed towards Platform 9, where he boarded a waiting train. Once he was out of sight, she approached the platform and noted from the indicator that the train was bound for Geneva. She also noted that he carried no luggage, nor the package he had collected at the jeweler's. That had been left, presumably, at Marcus Behrens.

After watching the train depart, she rang George Mason on her cellphone.

"What developments, Alison?" he anxiously enquired.

"I had quite an interesting morning," she replied. "Oleg Volkov made several calls in the city before taking a train to Geneva. He has just this minute left."

"Geneva?" her colleague queried. "Are you at the station right now?"

"I just watched his train pull out."

"Hang on a few minutes and I shall join you there. I am not all that far away, as a matter of fact; just along the Bahnhofstrasse."

"Did you visit Leutnant Kubler?"

"I intended to, but he is out on a call and will not be back until after lunch. We shall grab a bite to eat and visit the Polizei Dienst later. It is quite close to the station."

Alison Aubrey passed the brief interval before Mason's arrival by returning to the bookstore to browse the titles, choosing a paperback by Hermann Hesse, a Nobel prize-winning novelist she had long been interested in, if hardly read. George Mason complimented her on her taste in literature when he caught up with her just after midday.

"So what did our friend Volkov get up to this morning?" he asked, steering the young sergeant towards the station cafeteria, where they shared a ham-and-artichoke pizza.

"First thing he did on leaving the Storchen was to enter a sauna in the Altstadt. That left me somewhat at a loose end, but I did spend a quiet hour in the

Lindenhof listening to violin music before he re-emerged."

"Where did he head then?" an intrigued George Mason asked.

"He walked back down to the embankment, to a row of fascinating craft boutiques. I nearly lost him altogether in the narrow winding streets, but I caught up with him just before he entered a jeweler's named Ebnother."

"The old city is a warren of medieval alleys," her senior remarked. "I know it well."

"On exiting the shop with a large package under his arm, Volkov crossed the river and followed the Limmatquai towards Belle Vue. From there, he continued along Seefeldstrasse and entered a building with the name-plate Marcus Behrens."

"That sounds like one of those private banks Zurich is noted for," Mason said. "Leutnant Kubler will tell us more about it."

"He then went directly to the main station and bought a coffee and a newspaper, before boarding the Geneva express."

"My compliments, Alison," her colleague then said. "You have done very well."

"Quite a new experience for me," she replied, appreciating the compliment, "tailing a suspect round a foreign city."

"All grist for the mill," he rejoined. "And that's an interesting book you have there. I read *Siddartha* some years ago. Did you know that Hermann Hesse spent part of his life here in Zurich?"

"I was not aware of that," she said. "I shall enjoy it all the more."

"He lived in a house somewhere near the lake. On Schanzengraben, I think it was."

"That is quite a mouthful."

"German names often are," he explained, "because they string words together. Hauptbahnhof, for example, is really three words. *Haupt* means head; *bahn* means railway and *hof* can mean any large area, such as a courtyard, a city square or even a farm."

"You are a mine of information, George," Alison admiringly remarked. "But we can hardly sit here all day, pleasant as it is, parsing words while waiting for the train back from Geneva."

Mason returned an ironic smile at that remark, while glancing at his watch.

"I expect Rudi Kubler will be back at his office by now. Let us pay him a visit."

The police lieutenant was indeed back at his desk enjoying a salami roll and a glass of mineral water for a make-shift lunch by the time the Scotland Yard pair arrived at the Polizei Dienst. He rose from his place and greeted them warmly, nudging his unfinished snack to one side.

"Good to see you again, Inspector Mason," he said. "I trust the world has been good to you since our last meeting?"

"Obliging enough, on the whole," his visitor replied, "over the past two years or so since I was last in Zurich."

"You are always welcome here, Inspector," Kubler then said. "What can we do for you now?"

"First, let me introduce my colleague, Detective Sergeant Alison Aubrey," Mason said.

"Delighted to meet you, Sergeant," the Swiss officer said, offering his hand.

"All we really need," George Mason continued, "is some information. We are here in Zurich because of our interest in a certain Oleg Volkov, who is the subject of a major investigation in England."

"And the bird has flown to Zurich?" Kubler asked, with a quizzical smile.

"Temporarily, we believe. We think he is in Switzerland on - for want of a better word - a business trip. Sergeant Aubrey tailed him to a jeweler's named Ebnother on the shopping arcade known as Schipfe."

"I know the place you mean," the Swiss immediately replied. "My wife occasionally buys costume jewelry there."

"Is it a legitimate business?" Mason asked.

"We have had no complaints about it, I do know that," came the reply.

"Volkov has already been implicated in a major wine scam," Mason explained, "involving the use of fake labeling to pass off *vins ordinaire* as rare vintages."

"A not-uncommon practice, Inspector, regretfully."

"Decidedly," Alison chipped in. "We all want our plonk, no matter what the price, to be genuine plonk."

"Or our Chateau d'Yquem 1790 to be genuine Chateau d'Yquem," Leutnant Kubler pointedly added.

"We suspect that Oleg Volkov," George Mason then said, "together with an associate of his, is running either a protection racket or a joint criminal enterprise. On leaving the jeweler's, the suspect was observed carrying a large package which he eventually left at a firm called Marcus Behrens. We are assuming that he took some sort of rake-off from the business. What we should really like to know is whether Ebnother deals in fake, as well as genuine, jewelry."

Kubler carefully weighed his visitor's words and slowly nodded his head.

"That should not be too difficult to determine," he remarked. "Walter Ebnother handles a number of Tiffany products, mainly silverware. He owns a chain of shops, often in popular skiing resorts such as St. Moritz, Gstaad and Flims, and in major cities like Bern and Geneva."

"So any scam could be quite widespread?" Alison said.

"If your suspect was depositing money at Marcus Behrens, which is a private bank," the Swiss officer explained, "there could be substantial sums involved. The minimum account balance there is 250,000 francs."

George Mason whistled aloud

"How could we determine if the jewelry is genuine or not?" he asked.

"Every piece of genuine Tiffany silver, such as bracelets and necklaces, will be stamped with the number .925, to indicate the metal content. It should have a heavy feel to it. Fake Tiffany, which is also on the market, has a lighter feel."

George Mason pondered those remarks for a few moments, before turning to his colleague.

"You could pay a visit to Ebnother's, Alison," he suggested, "posing as a potential customer. A young woman looking at jewelry will not arouse suspicion."

"I would enjoy doing that," she enthusiastically responded. "I rarely have the opportunity to handle fine jewelry."

"Don't go overboard and buy something," Mason teasingly cautioned.

"On a police officer's budget, George?" she replied. "Are you kidding?"

Rudi Kubler could only smile at the humorous exchange.

"Call back here if you come across anything untoward," he advised, resuming his light lunch. "I shall be here at my desk doing routine work most of the afternoon. Good luck with your enquiries."

With that, the two visitors rose and took their leave, heading back to the riverside arcade known as Schipfe. George Mason walked a little farther on, to an antiquarian bookstore at the end of the arcade, while Alison Aubrey visited the jewelry store. Forty minutes later, they met up again for coffee at an embankment café.

"Leutnant Kubler was spot on," Alison said. "Ebnother stocks both genuine and fake Tiffany products. I could tell straight away by the feel of comparable items, even before examining the silver content."

"Did the proprietor seem suspicious?" her senior asked.

The detective sergeant shook her head.

"I did not see him," she replied. "He may have been in a back room, for all I know. An elderly woman showed me the items I requested and did not hover over me, anticipating a sale."

"In upmarket stores like that," Mason commented, "they give their well-heeled clientele plenty of leeway. They do not need to push sales."

"It is a much larger premises than it appears from the outside. The display cabinets extend well back, with a fascinating variety of products."

"So you had yourself a whale of a time, undisturbed?"

"I could have stayed there all afternoon," she replied, with a deft smile.

They sipped their coffee, served with a square of dark chocolate, while watching a university rowing crew head downstream.

"Leutnant Kubler will be very interested in your findings," George Mason said. "Time to pay him another visit."

They finished their drinks, settled the bill and soon covered the short distance to police headquarters. Leutnant Rudi Kubler was a little surprised to see them return.

"I would have placed a bet that Walter Ebnother ran a legitimate business," he remarked, as they took their seats facing his cluttered desk. "My wife Trudi will now be examining the items she has purchased there in the past."

"There is a fifty-fifty chance they will be genuine," Alison Aubrey observed, "from what I noted in the store."

"Let us hope so," the Swiss officer replied, with pronounced feeling, "and not only for Trudi's peace of mind."

"Keep this information under your hat for the time being," Mason urged, "until we get to the bottom of this whole business."

"I can suspend any appropriate legal proceedings in the short term," Kubler agreed.

"We shall give you the go-ahead in due course," Mason said. "What we really need now is a handle on the money."

"The account at Marcus Behrens?"

His visitor nodded.

"We need to know whose name is on the account," he explained. "It could be a certain Otto Steiner, assuming that Oleg Volkov is a mere errand boy for him. Alternatively, it could be a joint account Steiner-Volkov, if they are equal partners in crime."

The Swiss officer considered the matter carefully. After a few minutes, he said:

"I could ask the Kantonal Taxburo to do a special audit."

"What of your vaunted banking confidentiality?" Alison asked.

"Swiss law allows for transparency in cases where fraud, criminality or tax evasion is suspected," Kubler informed them. "Foreign clients are now required to pay any taxes due in their home countries before placing money in Swiss bank accounts."

"How long would a special audit take?" an intrigued George Mason asked.

"It could be completed within days," Kubler replied, "if the request comes through this office."

"So you will put that procedure in motion and inform us of the result by telephone to Scotland Yard, will you, Leutnant?"

"I shall be very happy to do so," came the reply. "We must ensure, by every means possible, that crime does not pay."

"Amen to that," Alison Aubrey said.

On leaving the Polizei Dienst, George Mason consulted with his colleague on her preferences for the remainder of the afternoon, feeling that they had already achieved a great deal so far that day and would not be able to catch up with Oleg Volkov until evening, assuming that he returned to Zurich.

"Would you care to visit the stores?" he enquired, aware of her interest in fashionable clothing.

Alison Aubrey demurred.

"I would much prefer to do some sightseeing," she replied.

"Since it is such a fine afternoon, how about a boat trip?" he suggested, directing his steps towards the lake.

"Fine with me, George," Alison said, increasing her gait to keep in step with him. "I am entirely in your hands."

"We would have time before dinner to visit Rapperswil, for example, at the far end of Lake Zurich."

"What are the attractions there?"

"The rose gardens, for one thing," he replied. "They should be just coming into bloom."

"Sounds good. I love roses."

"And there is a well-preserved castle, dating from the fourteenth century, overlooking the harbor."

The young sergeant gazed at him in amazement, while striving to match his quicker gait.

"How do you know all of this, George?"

"I glanced at a tourist leaflet at the hotel," he explained. "They have a selection of them in the foyer."

By now, they were approaching the end of Bahnhofstrasse, said to be Europe's most expensive street. The boat quay hove into view.

"That must be it," an excited Alison Aubrey said, indicating a large vessel at mooring.

On reaching the lakeside, they purchased return tickets at the kiosk and mounted the gangway to the foredeck of the *Schwyz*, so named for one of the three original cantons forming the Swiss Federation. It would depart at 2.45 p.m., giving them a few minutes' wait.

"The castle – which, incidentally, was built by an Austrian duke – is not the only historical site at Rapperswil," Mason said, as they occupied deckchairs to rest their feet.

"The Romans were there," Alison said, hazarding a guess.

"Spot on, Alison! Among other achievements, they rebuilt a wooden bridge over the bay, linking two sections of the city. The bridge was first constructed, according to the leaflet I perused, around 1500 BC."

"You are surely kidding, George," Alison remonstrated. "Did they know how to build bridges so far back?"

"I don't see why not," came the quick reply. "The Pharaohs built pyramids. The Celts built Stonehenge. There is a picture of it in the leaflet, which I unfortunately left in my room. It is quite a long, impressive structure."

"I intend to walk across it," his young colleague said, "in my very first encounter with Neolithic architecture."

"After, or before, we have climbed up to the castle?" Mason quipped.

"Either way suits me, provided there is refreshment in between."

"For that, we shall try the Fischmarktplatz, in the medieval center of Rapperswil. It should have a good atmosphere."

The boat's whistle sounded. Minutes later, it eased away from the quay and headed out in a fresh breeze towards the center of the lake, within view of extensive, well-kempt gardens reaching down to the southern shore, where the wealthier suburbs of Zurich were located.

*

On their return from Rapperswil by an early-evening boat named the *Uri,* apparently the sister-ship of the *Schwyz,* the two detectives freshened up in their respective rooms before going down to dinner. They sought out a table in a window alcove, from where they would have a good view of the restaurant in case Oleg Volkov returned there from Geneva. They scanned the elaborate menu, as the room began to fill with fellow-diners, including Chinese, Japanese and American tourists.

"A five-course dinner," was Alison's first reaction. "We should be able to do it justice, after all that sight-seeing we did this afternoon."

"You enjoyed it then?" her colleague rather superfluously asked.

"Wouldn't have missed it for the world," she replied. "You are a good tourist guide, George."

"What did you especially like?" he asked, smiling at the compliment.

"I loved exploring the narrow, cobbled alleys in the old quarter, with their quaint boutiques, colorful houses and unexpected twists and turns. They call it the Altstadt, same as here in old Zurich."

"Dating from the same era, no doubt."

"And I thought the Neolithic bridge was a wow. An amazingly robust structure, to have survived several thousand years."

"Indeed, Alison. The Neolithic peoples and the Romans evidently knew their stuff. And what about the roses?"

"They were just gorgeous, George. There must have been hundreds of different varieties. Gardens seemed to be everywhere."

George Mason smiled in acquiescence and studied the menu more closely.

"I shall start with minestrone soup," he said, after a while. "followed by sole meuniere."

"What exactly is that?" his companion asked.

"The fillet is coated with flour and fried in butter," he said. "Meuniere is French for miller's wife."

"Must be good then, being French. I think I shall start with the vegetable soup, followed by beef Wellington."

A waiter hovered nearby, stepping closer to take their order.

"And for the wine, sir?" he asked.

"A half-carafe of Australian shiraz," the detective said. "The Banrock Station, perhaps."

"Very good, sir," came the response.

As the waiter left, the two detectives glanced round the room, which was now about two-thirds full.

"Do you think our friend will show up, Alison?" Mason asked.

"Difficult to say, really," she rejoined. "Suppose he remains in Geneva and flies back directly from there?"

"It may not make any great difference what he does," her colleague said. "I would have liked to keep tabs on him for a while longer. On the other hand, we already have quite a lot on him with the wines and the jewelry. Time is on our side. If there are five courses to get through and service is slow, we shall be here until ten o'clock."

"If Volkov does not make an appearance, what do you intend to do, George?"

"In that event, I want you to return to London first thing after breakfast tomorrow morning," he said.

"By myself?" Alison asked, with a surprised look. "What are your plans for tomorrow?"

"I have some business to attend to in Germany," he said, rather evasively, not wishing to alert his colleague to his concerns regarding Otto Steiner, ahead of her invitation to a barbeque at her home.

"When will you be back at the Yard?" she asked.

"The day after tomorrow, most likely," he replied.

"Which part of Germany will you visit?"

"North-central Germany," Mason replied.

"Is it about the Europol exchange scheme?" she probed.

"In a manner of speaking," he cagily replied.

The soup arrived at that point, to start off a lengthy meal which occupied most of the evening. George Mason steered the conversation onto more general subjects. By ten o'clock, the suspect had not still appeared, so they assumed he would not be returning to Zurich that day. On rounding off a gourmet meal with coffee, they were ready to retire. The exertions of the day had caught up with them. Back in his room, Mason switched on the television and poured himself a nightcap from the mini-bar. On vaguely following the late news, his attention was immediately riveted by an item from Germany regarding the recent state elections. Results were being announced in alphabetical order. Sitting bolt-upright in his chair, he watched the screen closely for the result at North Saxony. Ilsa Weiss had just been declared president!

Chapter Eleven

Oleg Volkov was in a buoyant frame of mind as the express train, after making its last major call at Lausanne, skirted Lac Leman on its end-run to Geneva. He had spent a useful day so far. Walter Ebnother's chain of jewelry stores were even more profitable than the wine scam at Dinard. After depositing some of the proceeds at Marcus Behrens on Seefeldstrasse and entraining at Zurich Hauptbahnhof, he had broken his journey at Luzern and Bern to collect a cut from Ebnother branches in those cities, which profited from the tourist trade. Now enjoying a splendid view of the lake from his window seat, he reflected on his visit that morning to the sauna in the Altstadt. It had been just about the hottest such bathe he had ever experienced, the needle in the heat chamber hovering round 120 degrees Celsius.

The invigorating ordeal called to mind saunas he had taken at Kamp Spitz in the Black Forest, where he had first met Otto Steiner. Steiner's background in the Bad Harzheim police had impressed him, if only for the reason that he himself had once aspired to join the police in St. Petersburg but had been rejected, at five-and-a-half feet, as being too short in stature. He had eventually found his way to Germany, to take advantage of the country's economic upswing, finding sporadic employment in the catering trade. There had been good opportunities, depending on the season, in the Rhineland, the ski resorts of Bavaria and the North Sea island of Sylt. That his contracts were often terminated early because of his drinking problem did not cause him undue alarm. Chefs and waiters were in constant demand.

To open new avenues, he had taken advantage of European Union rules allowing free movement of labor to seek work in England. Private boarding schools, whose income stream was sometimes unpredictable, were a good option. They were often in pleasant rural surroundings and did not inquire too closely into one's background, being generally happy enough at finding service staff willing to work for modest wages. Short-term contracts also suited them, since they could be arranged to fit in with school semesters, thus avoiding expenditure on wages during the vacations. He fondly recalled, as the train neared its destination, his spell at Fletchers, Inkpen. The boys enjoyed his borscht soup, the kitchen staff were homely country people and the bar at Sparrowhawk Inn, with its chatty barman, was a welcome haven after a day's work.

His friendship with Otto Steiner had proved fortuitous. After his daily shift at Spitz, where he was employed as a sous chef, it had been his custom to visit Gasthaus zum Weintraub, near the Black Forest town of Unterkirnach, to spend the evening over a few steins of pilsner. The ex-cop was also a regular patron, sharing a taste for Cuban cigars. A request for a light provided the initial contact and they soon became regular drinking companions. The money-making schemes Steiner outlined had struck him as a bit far-fetched at first. But the ex-cop, who also claimed to have done jail-time, presented a glowing picture which proved very persuasive. The result, over the last few months, had been to greatly enhance his financial position. So much so that he, Oleg Volkov, a hitherto underpaid catering worker, had been able to place a deposit on a seaside villa at Sochi, in the Crimea. In the not-too-distant future, he would stage a triumphant return to his home country and impress his relatives and friends, while enjoying an early retirement on the Black Sea.

The train had now reached Geneva. Oleg Volkov figured that there was just enough time to make his last call of the day at the Ebnother branch near the Palais des Nations and deposit the proceeds in the local branch of Marcus Behrens before it shut its doors at six o'clock. On quitting the station precinct, he strode purposefully along Rue Versonnex to catch a city bus to his destination. He would afterwards visit one of the city's ethnic restaurants for dinner, having earlier booked a room for the night at the Ronsard, a five-star hotel on Quai de Mont Blanc. Otto Steiner would be well-pleased, he considered, with the way he had handled his part of the operation, when they next got together at the Bird in Hand pub, Holland Park.

*

Immediately after breakfast the next day, George Mason settled the hotel bill and accompanied Alison Aubrey to the train station, bidding her good-bye as she boarded the rail link to Kloten Airport, promising to catch up with her in two days' time. He then approached the kiosk to purchase a ticket to Hannover, bought a copy of the London *Times* to read on the way and headed to Platform 8. The Zurich-Hamburg express, calling at Stuttgart, Frankfurt and Hannover, was scheduled to depart in eleven minutes. Counting himself lucky to have such a short wait, he selected a compartment towards the front of the train, boarded and found an unoccupied window seat. He placed his valise on the luggage-rack, sat down and opened his newspaper, while musing on events of the previous day. Leutnant Rudi Kulber had, as on previous occasions, been very cooperative and helpful, especially by holding fire for the time being on any legal action against Walter Ebnother.

On reaching Hannover, he switched platforms for the connection to Bad Harzheim. Arriving there by mid-afternoon, he took a taxi to the police station, where he waited ten minutes until the polizei direktor was free. The German was quite surprised to see him.

"What brings you back to our neck of the woods, Inspector?" he genially enquired, offering his visitor a seat facing him.

"I happened to be in Zurich," Mason explained, "on the investigation you instigated into suspected racketeering. It was not much out of my way to call here, since I can catch the Eurostar service back to London from Brussels."

"There is a direct connection from Hannover to the Belgium capital," Weidman remarked.

"Your railways have a reputation for efficiency," his visitor said. "I left Zurich around 9 a.m. and here I am in Bad Harzheim."

"With something to report, I take it, from your demeanor?"

George Mason nodded.

"My colleague Sergeant Aubrey and I have been looking into the activities of Otto Steiner," he said.

"It is my Hildesberg colleagues who are mainly concerned about that, out of concern that some of their officers may be involved. There have been rumors, but nothing more than that."

"Steiner has an associate named Oleg Volkov," Mason continued. "Scotland Yard placed a roving bug in the pub they frequent most evenings. As a result, we have implicated them in two major enterprises, both criminal."

"Which are?" Hans Weidman asked, intrigued at the technology employed.

"One concerns the fake labeling of wine, which I telephoned you about."

The director returned a broad grin.

"Did you sample the bottle I let you hold on to?" he genially enquired.

"I certainly did," came the reply. "Caves de Montserrat 1850 was the best wine my wife and I have ever tasted. I thank you most heartily for the gift."

"Our embassy in London confirmed that they had received the bottles deemed genuine. They will make good use of them. Chancellor Merkel has scheduled a visit to your country in July."

"It should make for a good reception, Herr Direktor."

"And what is the other line you have exposed?" the German queried.

"Steiner and Volkov run what is shaping up to be a big operation in fake Tiffany," Mason informed him, "involving a chain of jewelry stores in major Swiss cities and resorts."

Hans Weidman whistled.

"I have alerted the Swiss authorities. Leutnant Rudi Kubler will initiate proceedings against the owner, Walter Ebnother, in due course."

"Keeping quiet about it until your enquiries are further along?"

"In the same way that you have not yet released details of Brendt Schulz's fate to the press."

"We have faithfully followed your guidance on that score," the other replied.

"So where is Kommissar Schulz now?" his visitor asked.

"At the morgue on the island of Sylt, Inspector."

"A most tragic incident, to lose one of your best officers in that manner. Tell me, Herr Direktor, who knew about Schulz's Europol exchange program?"

"Most everyone in the state of North Saxony," came the reply. "It was in all the media, when the announcement came through."

George Mason pondered that observation for a few moments, before saying:

"A large number of people, evidently, Herr Direktor. To narrow down the field, who would have known the deceased officer's schedule and itinerary on that particular day?"

"Evidently Otto Steiner knew it. We knew of it in this office. The Ordnungs Kommission will also have been briefed on it, as having oversight of general policing matters."

"Someone on the inside must have tipped off Steiner," Mason concluded.

"Otto Steiner had many contacts in the police service," Hans Weidman explained. "He was quite a popular officer and a natural leader. He recruited members of local police forces for a training camp, known as Spitz, in the Black Forest."

"What is that all about?" an intrigued George Mason asked.

Hans Weidman assumed an air of amused detachment.

"They like to dress up in military gear and do para-military exercises," he explained.

"White supremacists, perhaps?"

"Some people here believe so. They have been linked to the Norwegian group, Pro-Nordia, known for its racist views. But I think a lot of it is posturing and play-acting, in the main."

A junior officer, aware that an English visitor had arrived, at that point served afternoon tea. George Mason, who had scarcely eaten since breakfast, was very gratified by the courtesy. Tea with buttered scones, even if lacking strawberry jam and Devon cream, was just the ticket. The two officers partook of the refreshment in silence for a few minutes. On nudging his plate aside, Mason said:

"I believe you now have a new president, Herr Direktor."

The German finished a mouthful of scone, wiped his lips on a tissue and said:

"Indeed we do, Inspector. Ilsa Weiss won by quite a wide margin. Not my choice, however. I backed the Green Party. Their candidate was an environmental expert at the United Nations who decided he could achieve more by direct involvement in politics."

"He left Geneva to come to North Saxony?"

"He in fact grew up in Kassel, not very far from here. A sort of local boy, if you like, who would have realized his ambition but for the financial muscle of Freiheit Partei. They were able to outspend their rivals to a considerable extent, focusing mainly on television advertising."

"What were Ilsa Weiss's main qualifications for the job?" his visitor asked.

Hans Weidman leaned back in his chair and gazed beyond the detective, pondering the matter. Eventually, he said:

"She has a good track record in public affairs, being a leading member of the Ordnungs Kommission. And she is one ambitious woman. Winning the presidency has long been her main objective."

"What does Freiheit Partei actually stand for?" a curious George Mason asked.

"They have a nationalist agenda," came the reply. "They wish to abolish the euro and reinstate the

German mark. They, in fact, mirror many of the attitudes of the British Conservative Party, viewing the European Union as ideally a free-trade area, rather than as a federation on the American model."

Direktor Weidman refilled their tea-cups, offering his visitor the remaining scone, before saying:

"When it comes to the crunch with Herr Steiner, Inspector, his trial will take place here in Germany."

George Mason reacted in some surprise and momentarily stopped eating.

"How so, Herr Direktor?" he dubiously enquired.

"He is a German citizen who apparently killed a fellow-citizen on board a German vessel in German territorial waters."

His visitor finished chewing and slowly nodded his head.

"That last remark is the key to it," he agreed. "The waters off the island of Sylt are under German jurisdiction. But you lack one key element."

"What would that be?" Weidman enquired, with a slight frown.

"Motive," Mason replied. "There can be little doubt that Otto Steiner got rid of Kommissar Schulz in order to usurp his place at Scotland Yard. The question is why would he do such a thing? Could it simply be his love of police work?"

The German officer could only smile at the other's turn of phrase.

"You have a valid point there, Inspector," he allowed. "We are really in your hands. I am relying on you to provide sufficient motive for this heinous crime and cunning subterfuge."

"For cold-blooded calculation and nerve, it takes some beating, Herr Direktor. I shall give it my best shot and see if we can soon draw a line under this investigation."

"I have every confidence in you, Inspector," Hans Weidman said, in conclusion.

"At least, for the time being, you have useful information on his racketeering," his visitor said.

"A good piece of work, Inspector. I shall inform my colleagues at Hildesberg first thing tomorrow morning. I shall also alert the French police about the wine scam at Dinard, and I shall soon be in touch with Leutnant Kubler at Zurich Polizei Dienst."

On taking his leave, George Mason took a cab to Hotel Rheinfells, the comfortable inn where he had stayed on his previous visit to the spa town. On arrival, he phoned Adele to say that she could expect him home the next day. After resting a while, he set out to sample the local attractions, with the prospect of dinner, his first real meal of the day, later on.

*

On the Saturday. Detective Sergeant Aubrey, following her senior colleague's suggestion, invited the bogus kommissar to visit her new home at Henley-on-Thames. She gave the German instructions on how to reach the town by train from Paddington Station. He arrived shortly after midday, having spent part of the morning at the Maida Vale sauna, close to the police hostel. The young sergeant met him at the station, thinking she would give him a brief walking tour of the town before driving out to her suburban home. That would give her schoolteacher-husband Malcolm plenty of time to do what he liked doing best, organizing barbecues.

"You made it!" the unsuspecting young woman exclaimed, as he left the platform.

"I almost forgot to change trains at Twyford," Otto Steiner remarked. "Otherwise, I do not know where I would have ended up."

"Most likely at Oxford," Alison said.

They walked down to the river and along the embankment, pausing now and then to watch the oarsmen from Oxford University in training for the annual boat race against Cambridge, which took place on a London stretch of the river.

"Henley has its own Royal Regatta in July," she told him. "Thousands of visitors arrive for the five-day event, to watch the races and take part in the festivities."

"Why is it called the Royal Regatta?" her guest wanted to know.

"Because Prince Albert once patronized it," came the reply, "at some point during the nineteenth century. Somewhere around 1850, I think it was."

"Prince Albert?" queried the German.

"The consort of Queen Victoria," Alison replied. "He died quite young, of typhoid fever."

"That explains the Albert Memorial in London?" Steiner said.

"And the Royal Albert Hall, where the annual Promenade Concerts are held. You should try to attend one while you are in London."

"I probably shall, now that you mention it. I enjoy classical music."

They continued walking until they reached the five-arched stone bridge spanning the Thames. Alison Aubrey told him that it was a listed building, constructed in 1786, and that the tower of St. Mary's church, now visible above the roof-tops, was even older than that, dating from the sixteenth century. Her guest was suitably impressed.

"You have so much here of historical interest," he remarked. "I already made time to visit the Tower of London and Hampton Court."

"And now you are visiting historic Henley-on-Thames, for good measure!"

"Most grateful I am for your kind invitation," Steiner said. "It is ages since I enjoyed home cooking. I am looking forward to it."

"You are most welcome," she replied, leading the way at a good pace across the bridge and along the opposite bank, until they approached a large brick building set in spacious grounds reaching down to the river. The animated voices of children at play reached their ears.

"Looks like a girls' school," the German remarked, pausing ostensibly to buy ice-cream for them both from a riverside vendor.

"That is Notaries Academy," his host proudly announced. "One of the famous guild schools."

"What exactly are they?" her guest disingenuously asked.

"Seats of learning originally established by medieval craft guilds," Alison explained. "They are generally well-endowed, but also rely on fees paid by wealthy parents. Some of them have struggled a bit since the recession. People lost their jobs, investments tanked."

"I can appreciate that," Otto Steiner replied.

"There is a lot of traffic hereabouts," Alison said, noting the limousines and sedans on the driveway. "It could be some sort of open day."

"Let us take a closer look," he said, starting up towards the school.

The detective sergeant was a bit puzzled as to why he would want to do that, since he was not a prospective parent. But if he was genuinely interested in British education, as an important aspect of British life, why not, she considered? She fell in step with him as they neared the building, which he examined closely, the way a student of architecture might, noting where the dormitories were and the fire escapes, as well as the classrooms.

"I quite recently visited a guild school," she informed him, as they finally directed their steps back towards the station parking lot, where she had left her car.

"Is that so?" he enquired, in neutral tones.

"Fletchers, in the village of Inkpen, Berkshire," she informed him. "I was investigating the kidnapping of a student, which took place there a few weeks ago."

"How fascinating is that!" he declared.

"Inspector Mason and I are still working on the case."

"Have you come up with a suspect?"

Alison Aubrey was of a mind to tell him about a person known to her as Oleg Volkov. But, remembering George Mason's caution about keeping things under wraps for the time being, she did not name him. Instead, she shook her head.

"These enquiries take time," her guest replied, mock-consolingly.

"After the barbecue this evening," Alison then remarked, "my husband Malcolm will take you rowing on the river."

"I should greatly enjoy that," he replied. "But will there be enough time?"

"The last train to Paddington leaves Henley at 10.35 p.m.," she replied. "That should allow us plenty of time.

*

After lunch that same day, George Mason left his West Ruislip home and took the tube to Maida Vale, confident that Otto Steiner would be enjoying the hospitality of Alison Aubrey and her husband, whose barbecues were legendary. On arrival at the police hostel, he asked the warden, Rick Selby, for the master key to enter the appropriate room. Selby reacted in some surprise at the unusual request, maintaining that the German had been a model tenant, establishing good relations with the young cadets, while strictly observing house rules. That did not surprise the detective at all. The bogus kommissar's conduct had been unexceptionable in every way since arriving at the Yard, probably to avoid the slightest scrutiny.

On entering the bed sitting-room, which was kept very tidy except for a pile of laundry on the bed, his attention was arrested at once by a framed photograph on the bedside table. He crossed the room and peered closely at it. Although it was a much younger likeness, the subject was familiar. It was unmistakably Ilsa Weiss! Mason took the picture in his hands and held it up to the light from the window. He could then read the words *Liebe von Ilsa* in the bottom right-hand corner. His knowledge of German told him at once that the legend meant *Love from Ilsa.* He whistled aloud and sat down on the edge of the bed, to weigh the impact of this startling new piece of the puzzle. It put an entirely new complexion on the case, in that it seemed to imply that Steiner and Weiss were lovers!

Replacing the photograph, he examined the books on the shelf above the bed. The titles confirmed what Hans Weidman had told him about paramilitary training sessions at Spitz in the Black Forest. There were books on physical fitness, weight-lifting, firearms, white water rafting, dieting and a directory of Rhenish wines. The small library included a few titles of fiction, all in German, whose authors, apart from Gunther Grass, meant little to the detective. Otto Steiner, he mused, was evidently a person of broad tastes and many attributes. Even his criminal pursuits reflected as much. If George Mason was hoping to find a computer, which could later be used to extract evidence in the form of emails, he was disappointed. There was not even a laptop in the room. A quick rifle through the drawers also revealed nothing.

With a final glance at the photograph of Ilsa Weiss, he left Steiner's quarters, locked the door behind him and returned the master key to the warden, who was evidently hoping for some sort of explanation. George Mason merely cautioned Selby to say nothing about his visit that day and to act normally in his dealings with the German, to avoid arousing even the slightest suspicion on his part. On leaving the building, he took the tube to Westminster and called at Scotland Yard to telephone Hans Weidman about his startling new discovery. The officer-in-charge at Bad Harzheim police station, on answering his call, informed him that the director was not on duty that weekend. Monday would be the earliest opportunity to contact him. George Mason shrugged on hearing that, left his office and headed to the West End to buy theatre tickets. His interesting news would have to wait a few days.

Chapter Twelve

On Sunday evening, Oleg Volkov took the District Line tube to Kensington High Street, deciding to cover the remaining distance to Holland Park on foot, to take advantage of the fine weather. He was in a buoyant frame of mind as he at length entered the Bird in Hand, where he found Otto Steiner just finishing a pint of Flower's Bitter. On joining his friend, he paid scant attention to the two young women sitting a few tables away, seemingly engrossed in conversation.

"Good evening, Oleg," Steiner said, rising to his feet. "What will you have to drink?"

"The same as you're having," came the reply.

Steiner crossed to the bar, returning minutes later with two pints of beer with a good head of froth, which he set down on the table.

"What news from Switzerland?" he enquired.

"Everything went according to plan," Volkov informed him. "I called at several Ebnother outlets and deposited the proceeds in your account at Marcus Behrens."

"The branches in ski resorts can wait until the new season starts," his companion remarked. "Meanwhile, we have a new project to consider."

Oleg Volkov quaffed his ale contentedly. Steiner's projects were music to his ears, in that he would the more quickly pay off the mortgage on his villa at Sochi.

"Detective Sergeant Alison Aubrey was kind enough to invite me to a barbecue yesterday at her home in Henley-on-Thames," Steiner told him.

"A very upmarket place, Otto. You are evidently moving up in British social circles."

Otto Steiner smilingly brushed the notion aside, saying:

"What the invitation really signifies, my friend, is that I am fully accredited at Scotland Yard. My cover remains intact."

"That in itself is a remarkable achievement," the other said, with frank admiration.

They both raised glasses and drank to that.

"Alison Aubrey gave me a brief tour of the town," the ex-cop continued, "before the early-evening barbecue. Her husband, by the way, is a first-rate cook."

"What did he serve?" the sometime chef was curious to know.

"Prawns in lime juice, for starters. Followed by a very good approximation to a wienerschnitzel. Dessert was a type of sorbet Alison had prepared."

"The Aubreys certainly did you proud," Oleg commented. "But what about our new project?"

"I was just coming to that," the other said.

At that point, Janet Midler rose from her place and passed quite close to their table on her way to the restroom. The eyes of both men followed her.

"Nice piece of crumpet, that," Oleg Volkov remarked.

"Forget it, Oleg," Steiner said. "You are not in her league. Attractive, I agree, but she strikes me as a professional woman. I have been keeping half an eye on the pair. Not once, since you entered, have they glanced in this direction. Just a couple of birds on a night out. Not looking for guys."

Oleg consoled himself with his beer.

"It turns out, Oleg," his companion continued, "interestingly enough, that there is one of those fee-paying guild schools at Henley-on-Thames."

"You don't say so!" Oleg exclaimed.

Otto Steiner gave him a sly smile.

"It will be, as the British are wont to say, just your cup of tea."

"I am all ears," the other said, sitting bolt upright.

"It is a private boarding school for girls. By a stroke of luck, it was open day when we were in town. Alison and I mingled with prospective parents, so I could case the joint quite easily."

"How did Sergeant Aubrey react to that?"

The ex-cop returned an ironic smile.

"I think she was concerned that I might have an improper interest in young girls," he sniggered. "But she went along with it all right. To indulge me, I imagine, as her guest."

"You want me to do the joint?" his companion then asked.

"It should be a cinch," came the reply. "There is a fire escape leading down from the main dormitory, which is on the second floor. The windows will be left open on a warm evening."

"How can you be certain of that?"

Steiner returned what was almost a laser-stare.

"I experienced boarding school life myself," he rejoined. "They all adhere to a Spartan regime. They will leave windows open even in the thick of winter, for fresh air."

Volkov nodded in agreement.

"It was exactly that way at Fletchers," he said. "Do you wish me to apply for a catering job?"

"There will not be time for that. Make your way there in the early hours of the morning, when the pupils will be asleep. Enter the dormitory via the fire escape, grab the nearest girl and seal her mouth with duct tape so that she does not scream."

"But we shall not know who the victim's parents are," Volkov objected.

"The girl herself will soon tell us that. All the parents are well-heeled. Alison Aubrey told me that the school does not have bursaries for poorer students. Take Sam Snead along with you. He was very useful at Fletchers and will take you and the girl to his farmhouse on the Hampshire Downs. Negotiations with the parents will take place from there."

"You seem to have covered all the angles, Otto," his companion-in-crime commented.

"It should go smooth as clockwork, my friend."

"When?"

"Wednesday morning, around 2 a.m. Now sup your beer, Oleg. I wish to catch the seven o'clock screening of the new James Bond film at the Odeon, Kensington. Come along, if you like."

"Gladly, Otto. But we haven't eaten yet."

"We can eat later, perhaps at the pizzeria on the High Street."

"I would prefer Chinese," the other said.

"Either way," came the reply. "Let us get a move on, or we shall miss the start."

The pair quickly emptied their glasses and rose to leave. Whereupon, Janet Midler exchanged a significant glance with Helen Shaw. The detective sergeant from the Midlands and the constable from Sussex were alternating surveillance duties with the Middlesex officers, at George Mason's request. Midler, confident that the roving bug had been well-concealed, replaced her cellphone in her purse and slowly finished her glass of chardonnay. Helen Shaw paid a visit to the restroom. On her return, by prior arrangement with the barman, she removed Oleg Volkov's beer glass from the table and placed it carefully in her shoulder-bag. The two detectives then finished watching a nature program on television before getting up to leave.

*

On Monday morning, George Mason took the tube to St. James's Park and walked from the Circle Line station to Scotland Yard, aware that Abu Dhabi had recently put in a bid for the storied building.

According to a report in his newspaper, which he had hurriedly read over breakfast, they planned to turn it into apartments, offices and a luxury hotel. The Metropolitan Police would be moving to a new suite of offices on the Thames Embankment. He wondered, as he approached the building, what would happen to the famous museum holding artifacts of many of the notorious crimes which had taken place in London, including those of Jack the Ripper and John Reginald Halliday Christie, the serial killer active in the nineteen-forties.

Alison Aubrey greeted him cordially as he entered.

"Good morning, Inspector," she said. "Had a good weekend?"

"A very useful one, to say the least," he replied, without giving details. "How about you?"

"It was a great idea of yours," she remarked, "to have us entertain the kommissar. Malcolm really took to him and invited him to go rowing on the river."

"The barbecue was a success?"

"Absolutely," she replied, pouring him a mug of freshly-brewed coffee.

"I am glad it went well, Alison. You performed a very useful service," he said, leaving her puzzling over what exactly he meant by those rather cryptic words.

On entering his own office, Mason shut the door firmly, sat down and sipped his coffee while checking his emails. He then placed a call to Bad Harzheim.

"*Guten Tag, Inspektor*," came the upbeat voice of Hans Weidman.

"*Guten Morgen, Herr Direktor,*" George Mason said.

"You have something new to report?"

"You bet I have," Mason informed him. "I managed to effect a search of Otto Steiner's bed sitting-room at our hostel at Maida Vale. He has a framed photograph of a younger-looking Ilsa Weiss on the table next to his bed!"

His remark was followed by silence, before the German officer said:

"Many people in this state have photos of Ilsa Weiss. She is a well-known political figure."

"I do not imagine many of those likenesses are inscribed '*Liebe von Ilsa*'," Mason countered.

"Are you quite serious, Inspector?"

"Never more so."

"That puts an entirely new complexion on the case," Weidman remarked.

"When we met recently," Mason continued, "we were both at a loss for a plausible motive in the murder of Brendt Schulz. We may now have one."

"A love triangle?" the other queried.

"It is a bit of a long shot," Mason replied, "since we have no evidence linking Steiner to the death of Professor Weiss."

"What sort of evidence do you have, so far, may I ask?"

"We are very interested in his associate, Oleg Volkov, who seems to play second fiddle to Otto Steiner."

"You mean that Steiner gives the orders and Volkov carries them out?"

"Something like that, Herr Direktor. We are in the process of examining Volkov's DNA. At a shrewd guess, if we can link him to the death of Rainer Weiss, Otto Steiner will also be involved."

"Guilt by association?" Hans Weidman said.

"Possibly."

"What I still do not understand," the other continued, "is why Steiner would insinuate himself into the Metropolitan Police?"

"Perhaps because it was relatively easy for him to do so," Mason considered, "with his background in the service. Once here, he could virtually dictate the course of our enquiries. From the outset, Chief Inspector Harrington allowed him a great deal of initiative, in accordance with Europol policy, which also emphasized major crimes. Otto Steiner then proposed rivalry within the academic community, as a motive for murder."

"Were there plausible grounds for that?" the intrigued director asked.

"I must admit that there were. I pursued a certain Professor Ian MacQuarrie of Lothian University, an arch-rival of Rainer Weiss. But he was eventually cleared of suspicion."

Direktor Weidman demurred.

"You are proposing, Inspector, that Steiner's objective was to get Ilsa's husband out of the way, so that he could pursue his love affair with her unhindered, and that he aimed to cover up the crime by diverting the Metropolitan Police investigation?"

"You do not sound very convinced, Herr Direktor."

"I think there must be more to it than that," came the reply.

"At least, we have a working hypothesis for Steiner's unparalleled impersonation," George Mason replied. "I aim to build on it, the best way I can."

"I wish you the very best of luck, Inspector Mason," the other said. "You are certainly going to need it."

George Mason replaced the receiver and weighed his German colleague's remarks carefully. Minutes later, Bill Harrington summoned him for a morning conference.

"There is a new development in the case, Inspector Mason," Harrington began.

"There may be several," his colleague cryptically replied.

The chief inspector ignored that as a rhetorical remark, while saying:

"Sergeant Midler, of the Midlands Police, successfully placed a roving bug at the Bird in Hand, Holland Park last evening. Take this recording, Mason, and act in accordance with it."

"I shall do my best, Chief Inspector."

"Constable Shaw managed to retrieve Oleg Volkov's drinking glass from the same venue."

"To retrieve DNA from traces of saliva?" Mason asked.

Bill Harrington nodded.

"It is now with the forensic people. If they match it with DNA from the smaller bloodstain on the sauropod rib, we shall have a clear suspect in the death of Rainer Weiss."

"Excellent news, Chief Inspector," his colleague said, pocketing the tape-recording. "We are making good progress at last."

"Not before time, Mason," came the terse reply.

"What will be your reaction to leaving this building?" George Mason felt prompted to ask, before withdrawing.

His senior breathed a heavy sigh.

"After so many years," he said, "it will undoubtedly be a wrench. "Turning the old place into a hotel, though, is an interesting idea. It will be a huge tourist draw. Our overseas visitors will flock here hoping to see the likes of Sherlock Holmes!"

George Mason laughed aloud at that, as Bill Harrington's right hand hovered near his whisky drawer.

*

In the small hours of Wednesday morning, Sam Snead drove his Mercedes sedan through the deserted center of Henley-on-Thames and along the Thames embankment towards Notaries Academy. Next to him, in the front passenger seat, sat Oleg Volkov.

"Otto told me there was a small relief parking lot at the foot of the drive," Volkov said. "We shall leave the car there and walk up to the school."

The driver did as instructed. Minutes later, noting that it was a moonless night, they headed towards the main school building shrouded in darkness, save for a small blue lamp over the main entrance. Crossing the stretch of lawn fronting the school, they made for the fire escape near the rear of the building. As they began to mount it, Inspector George Mason and five uniformed officers from Oxfordshire Constabulary emerged from the shadows to confront them.

"Oleg Volkov and Sam Snead," the detective said, "I am arresting you for attempted kidnapping."

The nocturnal pair realized that flight or resistance was useless. The uniformed officers handcuffed them and led them to a police van parked behind the school. From there, they were taken to Paddington police station, to avoid alerting Otto Steiner of their arrest, and placed in separate cells. George Mason, satisfied with the night's work, went home to grab some sleep, returning to Paddington first thing the following morning. Volkov was brought to him in the interview room.

"You have nothing on me, Inspector," Volkov cockily observed. "We did not enter the school."

"On the contrary, Mr. Volkov," the detective replied, "we have quite a lot on you, and on your associate Otto Steiner."

Volkov's face took on an aura of frank disbelief.

"You are bluffing," he said, less self-assured.

"We have information linking you to the death of Professor Rainer Weiss at the Darwinian Institute on May 7 last."

Volkov's expression turned to one of alarm.

"I have no idea what you are referring to," he said.

"It has come to our notice," Mason continued, "that you were employed as a sous chef at Fletchers, Inkpen and at the annual dinner of the Darwinian Institute in Kensington. Can you deny that?"

The suspect fell silent, glancing downwards at the bare tile floor.

"May I smoke?" he asked.

"By all means," his interviewer said, crossing the narrow room to open the window.

Oleg Volkov drew out a pack of Kent cigarettes and a DjEEP lighter, lit up and considerately blew the smoke towards the open window. George Mason appreciated the gesture, withdrawing from his pocket the lighter of the same make he had retrieved from the copse near Fletchers that Brother Linus used for teaching plant ecology.

Volkov's eyes opened wide in amazement.

"Recognize it?" Mason asked. "It is a handy lighter. I use it myself for the occasional cigar I like to indulge in after dinner."

"It is a common brand," Volkov blustered. "Anybody could own one."

"It is not so common that I ever came across it before. We have, in fact, already taken fingerprints from this one, which will most likely match the prints you shall very soon give us. This inoffensive little object will place you at the village of Inkpen, Berkshire, from where student Timothy Tuttle was abducted some weeks ago."

"I deny it, Inspector. I know of no such place as Inkpen."

"On the contrary, you were well-known at Sparrowhawk Inn, and it would be quite a simple matter to have the barman identify you."

"May I have some water?" the perturbed suspect pleaded, stubbing out his half-finished cigarette.

The detective crossed to the table beneath the window and returned with a plastic container of spring water.

"Help yourself," he said, curtly.

For the first time, Oleg Volkov essayed a smile. He liked this officer's dry sense of humor. He also wondered how he had gotten so much on him. The seaside villa at Sochi was beginning to seem like a mirage. His eyes followed his interrogator, as the latter was suddenly called out of the room. The chief inspector was on the line from Scotland Yard.

"Walter Stopford just handed me the results of the analysis of saliva traces on the beer glass from the Bird in Hand," Bill Harrington jubilantly announced. "The DNA matches that of the blood sample on the sauropod rib. Oleg Volkov is our man, all right."

"Excellent, Chief Inspector," an inwardly elated George Mason said. "I am with the suspect at the moment. Place Otto Steiner under arrest as soon as he arrives at the Yard. He will smell a rat if Oleg does not contact him soon."

"On what charge, Inspector?"

"On suspicion of the murder of Brendt Schulz."

"I hope you have enough on him, Mason, to make that charge stick."

"Things are beginning to fall into place, Chief Inspector," his colleague assured him.

"They had better be!" Harrington boomed. "We shall look terrible fools at Europol if not."

George Mason returned to the interview room, where the suspect was puffing on his second Kent.

"The kidnapping of Timothy Tuttle is the least of your worries now, Mr. Volkov," he said.

The suspect drew heavily on his cigarette, returning a questioning look mixed with growing alarm.

"You will be charged at Westminster Crown Court with the murder of Rainer Weiss."

Oleg Volkov gasped aloud, realizing that the game was up. This man facing him, seemingly out of nowhere, had succeeded in linking him to two major crimes. His initial reaction was that Otto Steiner, to cover himself, had betrayed him. But that did not really seem plausible, unless the ex-cop wanted to keep all the financial proceeds of his various rackets.

"I wish to see my lawyer," the suspect then said.

"That can be arranged," came the reply. "But I would urge you to make a clean breast of things, Mr. Volkov. Turn Queen's Evidence and tell us all you know about Otto Steiner. It will go much easier for you in the end. You could get a lighter sentence."

"You are asking me, Inspector, to act as witness for the prosecution in the trial of Otto Steiner?" he asked, in disbelief.

"I am putting it to you, Mr. Volkov, that that is now your best chance. DNA evidence will help convict you of a crime warranting a life sentence without parole."

"I shall review the matter," the other cagily replied, "in conjunction with my lawyer."

"That is your legal right," the detective allowed.

The interview ended. Oleg Volkov returned to his cell, as Sam Snead was ushered into the room.

"You will be charged with attempted kidnap, at the very least, Mr. Snead," George Mason informed him, as they sat facing each other across the bare table.

"You may also be charged for your role in the abduction of Timothy Tuttle from Fletchers, Inkpen."

"I have no idea what you are talking about," Snead airily replied. "I wish to see my lawyer."

"We can easily ascertain, Mr. Snead, from Berkshire County records, that you own a farmhouse on the Hampshire Downs. That is where we believe young Tuttle was held captive, and where you would likely have taken your next victim had your little enterprise this morning succeeded."

"I wish to see my lawyer."

"That is your legal right," Mason replied, returning the uncooperative suspect to his cell.

He then left Paddington and drove indirectly to St. James's Park, making two routine calls on the way. It was late-morning by the time he arrived at Scotland Yard. Alison Aubrey stopped him as he was passing through the general office. He sensed that she was agitated.

"Bill Harrington has placed the kommissar under arrest!" she exclaimed. "Everyone one here is completely flabbergasted. They do not know what to think."

"The chief inspector surely had his reasons," George Mason evenly replied. "Get your things together and meet me in the parking lot in fifteen minutes. We are taking a short trip."

The young sergeant returned a questioning look, but her senior offered no explanation. He entered his own office, checked his emails and filed away some documents, before heading down to the basement parking lot. Sergeant Aubrey was waiting for him.

"We are going down to Inkpen," he announced, as he cut through heavy morning traffic to access the M4 motorway.

"There has been a breakthrough in the case, hasn't there, George?" Alison shrewdly surmised.

Mason merely nodded, focusing on his driving.

"Well, aren't you going to clue me in?" she then asked, a trifle petulantly.

Her colleague glanced towards her with a sly smile.

"You were part of the stratagem to help trap Otto Steiner," he said.

"Who on earth is Otto Steiner?" the incredulous sergeant asked.

"He is a former police officer from Hildesberg, North Saxony masquerading as Kommissar Brendt Schultz."

"So where is Brendt Schulz?" she asked in amazement.

"In the morgue on the North Sea island of Sylt. Director Hans Weidman and I are convinced that Steiner threw Schulz overboard from a Hansa Lines ship named the *Bremerhaven,* after it left Hamburg, in order to take his place on the Europol exchange program."

"You are quite amazing, George," Alison ruefully remarked. "You had me entertain a criminal suspect as an honored guest!"

"I assure you, Alison," Mason profusely apologized, "that it was the only way I could be sure of gaining undisturbed access to his private quarters at Maida Vale, which had some very interesting contents."

The young officer fell silent for a few moments, as she absorbed all this incredible information. Eventually, as the sedan turned onto the M4 slipway, she said:

"I accept your explanation, George, since you obviously felt it was necessary. One thing puzzles me, however. Why would this Otto Steiner, as you call him, effect such a daring subterfuge?"

"For one thing," came the reply, "he would not have expected his victim to wash up on Sylt. Had that not occurred, we should have been none-the-wiser about his true identity. As for his motives, Hans Weidman and I are working on that."

"The chief inspector must have something tangible on him to press charges," Alison remarked.

"He has indeed. Steiner is implicated with his friend Oleg Volkov in the kidnap conspiracy. While you were kindly showing him the sights of Henley-on-Thames, he was in fact casing Notaries Academy for the next abduction."

Alison Aubrey was unsure whether to laugh or cry. On recovering her composure, she said:

"How did you tumble to all of this?"

"By a roving bug placed at the Bird in Hand pub, Holland Park."

"You are a dark horse, Inspector," she remarked, settling into an ironic smile. "I never imagined you were so high-tech."

"I am not, really," he admitted. "It was Bill Harrington's idea. He is not as stuffy and pedestrian as one might think. He learned the technique from the F.B.I., who have apparently been using it for several decades."

Once on the motorway, sometimes dubbed the world's longest parking lot, they made good progress, reaching their destination just before one o'clock. George Mason headed slowly down the main street of the quaint Berkshire village and stopped outside Sparrowhawk Inn.

"Time for a spot of lunch," he announced, leading the way inside.

"A great idea, George," Alison said, recovering her equanimity as she accompanied him into the historic inn.

George Mason strode to the bar, as Alison Aubrey chose a table for two by a leaded side-window, rejoining her within minutes bearing two gills of the local brew.

"One reason for calling here," he said, setting the glasses down carefully and taking up the menu, "was to ask the barman if he would act as a witness in the trial of Oleg Volkov. But the original barman has apparently moved on. Got a job on a cruise liner, so the new barman says."

"He could be anywhere by now," Alison considered. "Even on the other side of the world."

George Mason returned a rueful smile as he quaffed his ale.

"Graham Thorpe at Fletchers will fill the bill," he said. "He owes me, for hiring an illegal alien. Now what is your fancy for lunch, Sergeant?"

"I think I should like the game pie," she replied. "It is not something one can readily find in the London area."

"I am for the brook trout," her colleague said. "It says here that it is caught locally, so it must be fresh."

"I love country food," Alison said, "especially in such pleasant surroundings."

They enjoyed a good meal together in a quiet atmosphere, as the pub regulars gradually drifted away. The young sergeant had gooseberry crumble for dessert, while Mason contented himself with coffee.

After lunch, they drove up to Fletchers, noting that crops were now well-advanced in the neighboring fields. Graham Thorpe was agreeably surprised to see them.

"What can I do for you, Inspector?" he enquired, inviting them into his office.

"We came to inform you that we now have a major suspect in the abduction of Timothy Tuttle," George Mason said.

"That *is* good news," the headmaster remarked, evidently relieved.

"It turns out to be none other than the person you hired as a temporary chef," Mason said. "The same person you omitted to mention as having left your service shortly before the incident."

Graham Thorpe shifted uncomfortably in his seat. Somewhat embarrassed, he said:

"You are referring, no doubt, to Oleg Volkov?"

George Mason nodded.

"A pity things turned out that way," the other continued. "He was in fact quite a good chef. The boys loved his borscht soup and potato pancakes."

"I doubt he will be spending much time in school catering," Alison Aubrey put in. "He is facing a long prison sentence."

"Deservedly so, no doubt," came the reply.

"We have also come to request you to act as witness for the prosecution in his forthcoming trial, which will take place at Westminster Crown Court," Mason explained.

"I shall do everything in my power to assist the course of justice," Graham Thorpe rather pompously replied.

"You need only testify that you employed Volkov here at Fletchers, and that it would take someone with knowledge of the school routine to be aware that Tuttle's class were out studying plant ecology at the relevant time."

"That will not be a problem," Thorpe replied.

"How is Timothy Tuttle doing?" Alison enquired.

"He has settled back into the school routine very well," the other said. "No long-term ill effects."

"Such as nightmares, panic attacks?" Alison Aubrey asked.

"Nothing of that kind, thankfully."

"It might interest you to know, Headmaster, that Oleg Volkov was recently detained while attempting another kidnapping at a guild school near London."

Graham Thorpe shook his head, regretfully.

"Private schools have to be increasingly aware of the danger of this sort of thing happening," he remarked. "We take all the precautions we can."

"Then I suggest," George Mason said, "that you get your staffing agency to vet applicants more thoroughly in future. Volkov illegally entered Germany from Russia, which is not a member of the European Union. Once in Germany, he could move unhindered into Britain."

The headmaster appeared suitably contrite.

"Hello, Mrs. Chips has generally served us well in the past," he maintained. "I have never had any complaints regarding ancillary staff they have recommended. I do hope this incident is a one-off."

"Let us hope so," Mason said.

"The Crown Prosecution Service will contact you in due course regarding the date of the trial," Alison Aubrey informed him, as the two detectives took their leave.

Chapter Thirteen

Shortly after George Mason reached his office the next day, he received a telephone call from Leutnant Rudi Kubler.

"Good morning, Inspector Mason," came the upbeat voice of the Swiss. "I have some interesting news for you."

"Good day, Leutnant Kubler," the detective rejoined. "Fire away. I can always use good news."

"The Kantonal Taxburo has completed its special audit of Bank Marcus Behrens," Kubler continued. "They discovered that an Otto Steiner has an account in his own name at their Zurich branch. There is no record of a joint account, to which he is party."

"When was the account opened?"

"About two years ago, Inspector. Regular transfers of substantial sums have since been made to the account of the Freiheit Partei at Hildesberg, North Saxony."

George Mason smiled knowingly to himself.

"That is most interesting, Leutnant," he remarked.

"I thought it might be," the other replied. "What I should like to know now is whether I can initiate proceedings against Walter Ebnother."

"Go ahead, by all means," George Mason replied. "Steiner and Volkov have both recently been placed under arrest here in London. The French police should also be alerted to the wine fraud at Dinard. I expect Direktor Weidman will do that soon enough."

"Thank you very much, Inspector Mason," Kubler said. "I appreciate it."

On replacing the receiver, George Mason crossed into the general office to fix himself a coffee. A pity, he considered, that Bill Harrington was out for the day at a conference in Brighton, since he would have preferred a meeting before contacting Hans Weidman at Bad Harzheim, to bring the chief inspector up-to-date on progress so far. Harrington liked to be kept abreast of developments. Instead, he exchanged a few pleasantries with Detective Sergeant Aubrey, who was writing up a report of their visit to Inkpen.

Back in his own space, he sipped his coffee while assessing the significance of Kubler's information. It seemed to him to throw an entirely new and unsuspected complexion on the case, aspects of which Hans Weidman would be more conversant with than he. On finishing his drink, he placed a call to Germany.

"*Guten Tag, Herr Mason,*" Hans Weidman greeted.

"*Guten Tag, Polizei Direktor,*" Mason replied, in his best German.

"How is your investigation into Otto Steiner proceeding?"

"Quite well, Herr Direktor," Mason replied. "He is currently in jail in connection with a kidnapping conspiracy."

"It seems he has more irons in the fire than I thought," Weidman rejoined.

"Just another of his financial enterprises," Mason said. "And I now have information from Zurich that there is a possible political angle to his crimes. Large transfers of funds have been made from his account to the Freiheit Partei account at Volksbank, Hildesberg."

"You don't say so, Inspector!" the other excitedly exclaimed. "That would go a long way to explaining how the party consistently outspent its rivals."

"It also puts Steiner's relationship with Ilsa Weiss in a new light, Herr Weidman."

"You mean that, in addition to a romantic involvement, he has been backing her political ambitions?"

"That conclusion seems inescapable and may give an additional reason for wanting Professor Weiss out of the way."

"Can you enlarge on that, Inspector?"

"Professor Weiss was due to appear at Winchester Crown Court on charges of selling fossils poached from the Gobi Desert. The Russian Embassy took a strong interest in the case, which would have caused a media sensation."

"It certainly would have done so here in his home state," Weidman agreed. "Professor Weiss was well-known here, even beyond academic circles, on account of his lively controversies."

"A trial would have reverberated strongly in North Saxony?"

"A scandal of that dimension would have seriously compromised his wife's bid for political office."

George Mason fell silent for a while, as he considered the German officer's remarks.

"You still there, Inspector?" the director asked.

"Excuse me, Herr Direktor," Mason hastened to reassure him. "I was thinking over what you just said. It would have been crucial for Ilsa Weiss, if she was going to win the election, to prevent that trial from going ahead."

"I see what you are driving at," Weidman replied. "You are suggesting that the presidential candidate conspired with Steiner to remove her husband from the scene, to give her a clear run in the upcoming election?"

"That would, more cogently than any love angle, or perhaps in addition to it, provide a motive for Otto Steiner insinuating himself into the Metropolitan Police."

"It would have been crucial for them to sidetrack the investigation, so that no hint of suspicion fell on themselves?"

"Exactly, Herr Direktor."

It was Hans Weidman's turn to fall silent.

"You still there?" George Mason asked, after a few moments.

"Forgive me, Inspector," the other replied. "But what you have just told me leaves me almost at a loss for words. We should need more than your suspicions to pin a murder conspiracy on our newly-elected president."

The Englishman thought about that.

"The two must have communicated with each other at some point along the way," he said. "You informed me earlier that Ilsa Weiss was well-informed about the Europol exchange program."

"She was instrumental in selecting Brendt Schulz as the candidate," Weidman replied.

"So she would probably have been familiar with his schedule?"

"Almost certainly. Ilsa Weiss, as a member of the Ordnungs Kommission, took a keen interest in the program. It was she who insisted that the exchange candidates spent their time on major crimes, rather than on day-to-day issues such as burglary and traffic violations."

"Since murders are a fairly infrequent occurrence in London," Mason said, "the conspirators could reasonably expect that the exchange candidate would be assigned to any recent incident of that type."

"Which is what seems to have occurred, Inspector, if your theory is correct."

"How calculating is that!" George Mason said. "We still need more proof."

"Would it be possible for you to check Ilsa's emails, Herr Weidman?"

The German officer thought for a moment, before saying:

"We could effect entry into her campaign office at night. It would involve enlisting the cooperation of her manager, Werner Hess, whom I know by reputation only."

"Tell him you suspect some irregularities in the conduct of the campaign," Mason suggested. "I imagine he will play ball, with the inauguration of the new president in prospect."

"Hess is a public-spirited individual," Weidman replied. "He will not want anything to tarnish the outcome of the election. I shall see what I can do and will contact you with the result."

"The best of British – or should I call it German? – luck," Mason said.

The polizei direktor essayed a nervous laugh.

"You have a nice sense of humor, Inspector Mason," he remarked, ringing off.

*

Oleg Volkov paced the yard behind Paddington police station, listening to the trains pulling in and out of the busy railway terminus. He had eaten a good breakfast of ham-and-eggs prepared by the duty officer and felt grateful at being allowed to take some exercise in the fresh air. His chief preoccupation was how he had ended up in this dire situation. He had assumed all along that Otto's schemes were watertight. How, therefore, had the police got wind of them? The more he considered the matter, the more convinced he became that the ex-cop from Hildesberg had betrayed him. He could then pocket the entire proceeds of their various enterprises and decamp to some Latin American country which did not have an extradition treaty with Britain. He was probably there now, sunning himself on some

Atlantic beach, aware that his associate had been arrested and might well talk. Yesterday afternoon, following Inspector Mason's visit, he had discussed his situation with his lawyer, Charles Braithwaite, who did not rate his chances of acquittal in any murder trial.

On returning to his cell after an hour's exercise, he spent the time reading a soccer magazine the duty officer had obligingly passed to him. He noted with satisfaction that the team he had supported in Germany, Munchen Gladbach, had finished the season top of its division. It was not in the same league as Bayern Munich, a team often qualifying for European competitions, but he took a special interest in its progress from having occasionally provided catering services in the executive suite.

In so doing, he had often got into conversation with the team manager and the owners of the club, who treated much like a personal friend. Around mid-morning, he received a visitor.

"Good morning, Mr. Volkov," George Mason greeted, on entering the cell.

Oleg merely nodded in response.

"Have you thought over carefully what we discussed yesterday?" the detective asked.

"I have given it a great deal of thought," came the reply.

"Did you consult your lawyer?"

"Charles Braithwaite of Calder, Braithwaite and Hays came yesterday. He recommended that I turn Queen's Evidence."

"And have you decided to do just that?" Mason asked.

The Russian nodded.

"I have little alternative," he replied, thinking that loyalty to Otto Steiner was now misplaced. He would look out for himself.

"A smart decision," Mason remarked. "Agents of the Crown Prosecution Service will visit you in the near future to take your statement on what you know of the crimes of kidnapping and murder in which you and Otto Steiner took part. I advise you to be as forthcoming as possible and include incidents at other guild schools, such as Silk Merchants and Cornmillers."

"I am willing to play ball," the other quickly assured him, "if it will mean a lesser sentence."

"There can be no guarantee of that, Mr. Volkov. It depends very much on the trial judge. But there are some recent precedents in your favor."

The suspect mulled over that observation for a few moments, before saying:

"I shall cooperate fully with the prosecution, Inspector."

"I am interested in your motives," the detective then said. "How did you come to get involved in all this?"

"Mainly for money," came the unhesitant reply. "I planned to buy a villa at Sochi and take early retirement there. I have, in fact, already made the initial deposit."

"How did you come to team up with Otto Steiner?"

"We first met at a training camp in the Black Forest. He outlined various money-making schemes over drinks at a country inn. I opted to go along with them."

"Even if it meant committing murder?"

"I am afraid so, Inspector. I was tempted by his offer of fifty thousand pounds."

George Mason shook his head in regret that a life could be bought so easily; yet he knew of similar crimes committed for as little as a few thousand pounds, by professional hit men.

"Did you ever meet a woman named Ilsa Weiss?" he then asked.

Oleg Volkov shook his head.

"The name means nothing to me," he replied.

"Were you aware of your associate's interest in politics?"

"We never discussed politics, in any shape or form. Otto and I were mainly interested in soccer. I supported Munchen Gladbach, while he backed Hannover. It would surprise me to know of his involvement in politics. I never trusted politicians. I have no time for them."

George Mason mulled over those remarks. There was nothing, it seemed to him, that Volkov could reveal at trial of the activities of Steiner and Weiss. What would emerge, under Queen's Evidence, was Steiner's role in the death of Professor Weiss, but not his motives. There would be nothing to link Ilsa to that scenario, unless Hans Weidman managed to uncover something on his home turf.

"Later today," he then told the suspect, before leaving, "you will be transferred to Wormwood Scrubs pending trial at Westminster Crown Court."

The sometime chef turned a few shades paler on hearing that.

"Do not be unduly alarmed," his visitor said. "The meals are quite good and they have better facilities than these local jails. There is a well-stocked library, workrooms and adequate recreation facilities."

"I shall be thankful for small mercies," the other rejoined, with a wan smile.

With that, the detective left Paddington. On his return to Scotland Yard, he stopped off at Kensington to call on the curator of the Darwinian Institute. Leonard Kidd was pleasantly surprised to see him. He invited his visitor into his study, where he proudly showed off the museum's latest acquisition.

"This is the skull of a horned dinosaur, Inspector," he said. "It lived in North America over one hundred million years ago. We are very fortunate to have come by it."

George Mason inspected the four-inch fossil closely.

"It seems to have been a very small creature," he remarked, recalling the terrifying predators in *Jurassic Park*.

"It is a popular misconception," the curator said, "originating in the movies, that all dinosaurs were large creatures. Many of them were in fact quite small."

"Its name?"

"Aquilops americanus."

"Most interesting, Mr. Kidd," Mason allowed, recalling the controversy over *homo caledoniensis*.

"This is surely not just a courtesy visit, Inspector?" the other queried.

"Indeed not, Mr. Kidd. I called to let you know we now have a firm suspect in the death of Professor Rainer Weiss."

"Excellent news, Inspector," the curator said.

"We have arrested an individual who assisted with the catering for your annual dinner on May 7 last. His name is Oleg Volkov."

"I seem to recall hiring someone of that name."

"We should like you to testify in court that Volkov was at these premises on the night in question."

"I can certainly do that," the curator replied. "It was a dreadful crime which gave unwelcome publicity to our institute. Museum visits by the general public have dropped off since then. I expect they will pick up again over the summer months and into the autumn, when we tend to get visits by school groups."

"Kids love dinosaurs," George Mason remarked. "In fact, they would treat something like this Aquilops here almost as a kind of pet."

The curator smiled at that observation.

"What news of the professor's widow?" he then asked. "How has she taken things?"

"Very much in her stride, I believe," his visitor replied. "She has just been elected president of the state of North Saxony."

"Indeed?" came the reply. "She must be one resilient woman."

"That is my impression, too, Mr. Kidd."

"I met her briefly at the funeral reception," Leonard Kidd remarked. "She struck me as unusually calm and self-possessed, in the circumstances."

"I too met Ilsa Weiss very briefly on that occasion," the detective said. "I formed a similar impression."

"The paleontology scene will be much less vibrant without Rainer Weiss. He was a very high-profile personality. And Wessex University will be hard put to replace him."

"I do not doubt that," George Mason replied.

"Can I offer you some small refreshment, Inspector, or a tour of the museum, before you go?"

"Thank you, no," his visitor replied. "It is very kind of you, but I must get back to the office. Good day to you, Mr. Kidd."

"Good day, Inspector Mason."

*

Two days later, George Mason received a telephone call from Bad Harzheim around mid-morning.

"Good news, Inspector Mason," Hans Weidman said. "With the aid of Werner Hess, we gained access to the campaign headquarters at Hildesberg."

"You managed to access emails on the office computer?" Mason asked.

"We did indeed, Inspector. And we have retrieved material that could link Ilsa Weiss to the deaths of both Brendt Schulz and Rainer Weiss."

"Can you expand on that, Herr Direktor?" the jubilant detective asked.

"We found two messages sent by Otto Steiner. The first reads: *Danke fur den Fahrplan des Schulz. Ich habe bestellt eine Kabine am Bremerhaven am selben Datum – Liebe, Otto.*"

"If my German serves me well," Mason replied, "it reads: Thank you for Schulz's travel schedule. I have booked a cabin on the *Bremerhaven* for the same date."

"Very good, Inspector Mason," the other complimented. "You have a good grasp of the German language."

"Thank you, Polizei Direktor   That email definitely links Steiner to the relevant Hansa Lines voyage."

"There is more," Weidman added. "On May 8, she received another message from Steiner. It read: *Alles in Ordnung. Ich habe billette fur den Agatha Christie beim Apollo Theater verkauft. – Otto.*"

"Everything in order. I have booked tickets for the Agatha Christie play at Apollo Theater – Otto."

"Very well done, Inspector. I checked the theater program on-line. The Agatha Christie play was presented during the week following Rainer Weiss's funeral."

"I got the impression at the reception, mainly from body language, that the two knew each other, although Steiner denied any personal contact with the Weisses."

"It seems your hunch was correct," Weidman said.

"That email reveals a lot, but it is too cryptic to be used as evidence in a court of law. 'Everything in order' could refer to the death of Professor Weiss or to the theater booking. You probably have enough to charge Ilsa Weiss in the Schulz case, but perhaps not enough to involve her in her husband's death. Not unless Steiner turns Queen's Evidence."

"I think that would be very unlikely, Inspector Mason, from what I know of him."

"In any event, we have the goods on him here, Herr Weidman. Oleg Volkov has agreed to testify for the prosecution."

"In that case, it will be better to try Steiner in your court, rather than in ours."

"I think the due procedure would be to try him first here in England, where we have a good chance of success, and follow it up with a trial in Germany. Justice must be served in both countries."

"It will be as you recommend, Inspector. We shall meanwhile move against Ilsa Weiss."

"Where might she be now?"

"On her way to the Stadthaus, I imagine, for the inauguration ceremony."

"How intriguing is that, Herr Direktor!" George Mason exclaimed.

*

Ilsa Weiss rose early that morning, showered and took a light breakfast at her home in the suburb of Unterwalden. She then summoned her hairdresser, who carefully arranged her coiffure before she donned a new business suit, admiring its chic lines in the wardrobe mirror. She then added some items of jewelry, to enhance the overall effect, while pinning a small party badge to her lapel. At just turned ten-thirty, her campaign manager Werner Hess arrived to drive her to the Stadthaus for a ceremony due to start promptly at eleven o'clock. He felt rather uneasy at Direktor Weidman's request the other day to inspect the office computer, but he dismissed his misgivings in the excitement of the morning's events. This would form the crowning achievement of months of dedicated work on behalf of Freiheit Partei, work that he felt sure would land him a senior salaried position in the new administration.

The successful candidate greeted him warmly as he arrived. Within minutes, they were on their way to the center of Hildesberg. Heading slowly down the main street, hung with bunting, they were greeted by an enthusiastic crowd of supporters and sundry onlookers, many waving flags. Heralding their arrival, a brass band played military marches near the foot of the flight of stone steps leading up to the Stadthaus. Civic dignitaries were there to greet her. As Ilsa Weiss and Werner Hess stepped out of the parked car to a cheering reception, police sirens obtruded jarringly onto the festive scene. The mayor and his entourage immediately checked their stride and held back. Cheering ceased, as the crowd shrank back from the base of the steps. Television cameramen and newspaper reporters closed in, watching in amazement as two squad cars came to a screeching halt just meters away.

Hans Weidman immediately stepped out of the lead car accompanied by two uniformed officers. Ilsa's jaw dropped as he approached; her usually calm gaze betrayed panic.

"I am apprehending you, Frau Weiss," the police director said, "on suspicion of complicity in the death of Kommissar Brendt Schulz."

The brass band abruptly aborted the military march, while the crowd melted back in bewilderment and disbelief, as the uniformed officers escorted the president-to-be to the waiting vehicle. Werner Hess fought back tears as the squad car quickly pulled away from the anticlimactic scene. His abiding memory was of his cherished candidate glancing wanly towards him from the vehicle's rear window. As he headed back towards the campaign office, to tie up loose ends, he consoled himself with thinking how much worse it would have been had Ilsa Weiss already been installed as their new president. By default, that office would now devolve to the Greens.

Made in the USA
Columbia, SC
24 March 2018